Praise for The Shipping News

Winner of the 1994 Pulitzer Prize for Fiction, the 1993 National Book Award for Fiction, the *Irish Times* International Fiction Prize, and the *Chicago Tribune* Heartland Award.

Named one of the notable books of the year
by *The New York Times*.

"Strikingly original, richly energetic . . . a stunning book, full of magic and portent."
—Douglas Glover, *The Boston Sunday Globe*

"*The Shipping News* is that rare creation, a lyric page-turner."
—Stephen Jones, *Chicago Tribune*

"The writing is charged with sardonic wit—alive, funny, a little threatening; packed with brilliantly original images . . . and, now and then, a sentence that simply takes your breath away."
—Bruce Allen, *USA Today*

"E. Annie Proulx's stunning, big-hearted *The Shipping News* thaws the frozen lives of its characters and warms readers."
—Roz Spafford, *San Francisco Examiner & Chronicle*

"Ms. Proulx blends Newfoundland argot, savage history, impressively diverse characters, fine descriptions of weather and scenery, and comic horseplay without ever lessening the reader's interest."
—*The Atlantic*

"Vigorous, quirky . . . displays Ms. Proulx's humor and her zest for the strange foibles of humanity."
—Howard Norman, *The New York Times Book Review*

"An exciting, beautifully written novel of great feeling about hot people in the northern ice."

The Shipping News . . . is a wildly comic, heart-thumping romance. . . . Here is a novel that gives us a hero for our times."
—Sandra Scofield, *The Washington Post Book World*

Praise for <u>Postcards</u>

"A rich, dark and brilliant feast of a book . . . A novel that feels like a fifth or sixth, not a first. This richly talented writer announces with *Postcards* that we had better, from now on, be listening for her voice . . . astonishingly accomplished."
—Frederick Busch, *Chicago Tribune*

"Story makes this novel compelling; technique makes it beautiful."
—David Bradley, *The New York Times Book Review*

"Superb . . . *Postcards* marks Proulx as a gifted prose stylist who renders her characters on the page to mesmerizing effect."
—Michael Upchurch, *San Francisco Chronicle*

"E. Annie Proulx's *Postcards* triumphantly delivers."
—Geoffrey Stokes, *The Boston Sunday Globe*

Also by E. Annie Proulx

The Shipping News
Postcards

E. ANNIE PROULX

HEART SONGS
AND
OTHER STORIES

SCRIBNER PAPERBACK FICTION
PUBLISHED BY SIMON & SCHUSTER
NEW YORK LONDON TORONTO SYDNEY TOKYO SINGAPORE

SCRIBNER PAPERBACK FICTION
Simon & Schuster Inc.
Rockefeller Center
1230 Avenue of the Americas
New York, NY 10020

SCRIBNER PAPERBACK FICTION and design
are trademarks of Simon & Schuster Inc.

Designed by Deirdre C. Amthor

Manufactured in the United States of America

3   5   7   9   10   8   6   4   2

Library of Congress Catalog Card Number 89-45705
ISBN 0-02-036075-4

The following stories appeared in somewhat different form in: *Gray's Sporting Journal,* "Stone City" copyright © 1979; *Esquire,* "The Wer-Trout" copyright © 1982; *Harrowsmith,* "On the Antler" copyright © 1983; *Gray's Sporting Journal,* "The Unclouded Day" copyright © 1985; *Esquire,* "Heart Songs" copyright © 1986; *Ploughshares,* "A Run of Bad Luck" copyright © 1987; *The Atlantic,* "A Country Killing" copyright © 1994; *Esquire,* "Negatives" copyright © 1994.
The author gratefully acknowledges permission to reprint excerpts from: *The Golden Casket* by Wolfgang Bauer, English translation copyright © 1964 by Harcourt Brace Jovanovich, Inc., reprinted by permission of the publisher; and from *Love and Protest,* edited and translated by John Scott, copyright © 1974 by André Deutsch, Ltd., reprinted with permission of the publisher.

Contents

On the Antler

HAWKHEEL'S face was as finely wrinkled as grass-dried linen, his thin back bent like a branch weighted with snow. He still spent most of his time in the field and on the streams, sweeter days than when he was that half-wild boy who ran panting up the muddy logging road, smashing branches to mute the receding roar of the school bus. Then he had hated books, had despised everything except the woods.

But in the insomnia of old age he read half the night, the patinated words gliding under his eyes like a river coursing over polished stones: books on wild geese, nymph patterns for brook trout, wolves fanning across the snow. He went through his catalogues, putting red stars against the few books he could buy and black crosses like tiny grave markers against the rarities he would never be able to afford—Halford's *Floating Flies and How to Dress Them,* Lanman's *Haw-Ho-Noo,* Phillips' *A Natural History of the Ducks* with color plates as fine as if the wild waterfowl had been pressed like flowers between the pages.

His trailer was on the north bank of the Feather River in the shadow of Antler Mountain. These few narrow acres were all that was left of the home place. He'd sold it off little by little since Josepha had left him, until he was down to the trailer, ten spongy acres of river bottom and his social security checks.

Yet he thought this was the best part of his life. It was as if he'd come into flat water after half a century and more of running the rapids. He was glad to put the paddle down and float the rest of the way.

He had his secret places hidden all through Chopping County and he visited them like stations of the cross; in order, in reverence and in expectation of results. In late May he followed the trout up the narrow, sun-warmed streams, his rod thrusting skillfully through the alders, crushing underfoot ferns whose broken stems released an elusive bitter scent. In October, mists came down on him as he waded through drenched goldenrod meadows, alert for grouse. And in the numb silence of November Hawkheel was a deer hunter up on the shoulder of Antler Mountain, his back against a beech while frozen threads of ice formed on the rifle's blue metal.

The deer hunt was the end and summit of his year: the irrevocable shot, the thin, ringing silence that followed, the buck down and still, the sky like clouded marble from which sifted snow finer than dust, and the sense of a completed cycle as the cooling blood ran into the dead leaves.

Bill Stong couldn't leave things alone. All through their lives there had been sparks and brushfires of hatred between Hawkheel and him, never quite quenched, but smoldering until some wind fanned up the flames.

In school Hawkheel had been The Lone Woodsman, a moody, insubordinate figure prowling the backcountry. Stong was a wiseacre with a streak of meanness. He hunted with his father and brothers and shot his first buck when he was eleven. How could he miss, thought woman-raised Hawkheel bitterly, how, when he sat in a big pine right over a deer trail and his old man whispered, "Now! Shoot now!" at the moment?

Stong's father farmed a little, ran a feed store and got a small salary to play town constable. He broke up Saturday-night dance fights, shot dogs that ran sheep and sometimes acted as the truant officer. His big, pebbled face was waiting for Hawkheel one school morning when he slid down the rocks to a trout pool.

"Plannin' to cut school again? Well, since your old man's not in a position to do it for you, I'm going to give you a lesson you'll remember." He flailed Hawkheel with a trimmed ash sapling and then drove him to school.

"You don't skip no more school, buddy, or I'll come get you again."

In the classroom Bill Stong's sliding eyes told Hawkheel he had been set up. "I'll fix him," Hawkheel told his sister, Urna, at noon. "I'll think up something. He won't know what hit him when I'm done." The game began, and the thread of rage endured like a footnote to their lives.

In late October, on the Sunday before Stong's fifteenth birthday, an event that exposed his mother's slovenly housekeeping ways took his family away.

Chopping County farmers soaked their seed corn in strychnine to kill the swaggering crows that gorged on the germinating kernels. One of the Stongs, no one knew which one, had mixed the deadly solution in a big roasting pan. The seed was sown and the unwashed pan shoved beneath the blackened iron griddles on the pantry floor where it stayed until autumn hog butchering.

The day was cold and windy, the last of summer thrown up into the sky by turbulent air. Stong's mother pulled out the pan and loaded it with a pork roast big enough to feed the Sunday gathering of family. The pork killed them all except Bill Stong, who was rolling around in Willard Iron's hayloft on a first shameful adventure. The equation of sex and death tainted his adolescent years.

As Stong grew older, he let the farm go down. He sat in the feed store year after year listening in on the party line. His sharptongued gossip rasped at the shells of others' lives until the quick was exposed. At the weekend dances Stong showed up alone, never dancing himself, but watching the women gallop past, their print blouses damp with sweat under the arms, their skirts sticking to their hot legs. At night he walked through town seeing which ones left the window shades up. He went uninvited to church suppers and card parties, winked out juicy tales and stained the absent with mean innuendo. Often his razor tongue stropped itself on the faults and flaws of his dead parents as though he had come fresh from a rancorous argument with them, and at other times he called them saints in a tearful voice.

Stong caught Hawkheel with petty tricks again and again. After Hawkheel started farming, once or twice a year he found the mailbox knocked over, water in the tractor's gas tank or the gate opened so the cows got onto the highway. He knew who'd done it.

Still, he kept on buying grain at the feed store until Stong told him about Josepha. Stong's eyes shone like those of a greedy barn cat who has learned to fry mice in butter.

"Hell, everybody in town knows she's doin' it but you," he whispered. He ate Hawkheel up with his eyes, sucked all the juice out of his sad condition.

It was cold in the store and the windows were coated with grain dust. Hawkheel felt the fine powder between his fingers and in his dry mouth. They stared at each other, then Stong scurried out through the chilly passageway that led to the house.

"He's got something coming now," said Hawkheel to Urna. "I could wire him up out in the woods and leave him for the dogs. I could do something real bad to him any time, but I want to see how far he goes."

Stong had sour tricks for everybody. Trade dropped away at the feed store, and there were some, like Hawkheel, who spat when they saw the black pickup heading out of town, Stong's big head turning from side to side to get his fill of the sights before the woods closed in.

For a long time Urna made excuses for Stong, saying that his parents' death had "turned" him, as though he were a bowl of milk gone sour in thundery weather. But when Stong told the game warden there was a summer doe in her cellar she got on the phone and burned Hawkheel's ear.

"Leverd, what kind of a man turns in his neighbor over some deer meat he likes to eat just as good as anybody?"

Hawkheel had an answer, but he didn't give it.

·   ·   ·

A few years after Josepha left, Hawkheel began to slide deep
into the books. He was at Mosely's auction hoping the shotguns
would come up early so he could get out of the crowd and take
off. But it dragged on, hundreds of the old lady's doilies and
quilts going one by one to the summer people. Hawkheel poked
through the boxes on the back porch, away from the noise. A
book called *Further Adventures of the One-Eyed Poacher*
sounded good and he dipped into it like a swallow picking mosquitoes off the water, keeping one ear on the auctioneer's patter.
He sat on the broken porch glider and read until the auctioneer,
pulling the crowd behind him like a train, came around to the
back and shouted "Who'll give me five dollars for them boxes a
books!"

Surrounded in his trailer by those books and the hundreds he'd
added to them over the decades, Hawkheel enjoyed his solitude.

Stong, too, was more and more alone up at the store. As he got
older, his trade dwindled to a few hard-pressed farmers who still
bought feed from him because they always had and because
Stong carried them until their milk checks came in. Listening in
on the phone wasn't enough now; he interrupted conversations,
shouting "Get off the line! I got a emergency."

"You ask me," said Urna to Hawkheel, "he's funny in the head.
The only emergency he's got is himself. You watch, they'll find
him laying on the kitchen floor some day as stiff as a January
barn nail."

"When I get through with him," said Hawkheel, "he'll be stiff,
all right."

Stong might have fallen to the cold kitchen linoleum with an
iron ringing sound, but in his sixties his hair turned a fine plat-
inum white and his face thinned to show good bones. It was a
time when people were coming into the country, buying up the
old farmhouses and fields and making the sugarhouses into
guest cottages.

"Bill, you look like a character out of a Rupert Frost poem,"
said the woman who'd bought Potter's farm and planted a thousand weedy birches on prime pasture. The new people said

Stong was a character. They liked his stories, they read morals into his rambling lies and encouraged him by standing around the feed store playing farmer—buying salt blocks for the deer, sunflower seeds for the bluejays and laying mash for the pet chickens they had to give away each fall.

Stong set his tattered sails to catch this changing wind. In late life he found himself admired and popular for the first time, and he was grateful. He saw what the summer people liked, and to please them he carried armloads of canning jars, books, tools and other family goods down from the house to the store. He arranged generations of his family's possessions on the shelves beside the work gloves and udder balm. He filled the dusty window with pieces of old harness, wooden canes and chipped china.

In autumn he laid in ammunition for the summer men who came back for their week of deer hunting. The sign in his window read GUNS BLUE SEAL FEED WINE ANTIQUES, a small part of what he offered, for all his family's interests and enterprises were tangled together on the shelves as if he had drawn a rake through their lives and piled the debris in the store.

"They say," said Urna, "that he's cleaned out everything from kettles to cobwebs and put a price tag on it. You know, don't you, that he's selling all them old books his grandfather used to have. He's got them out there in the barn, higgledy-piggledy where the mice can gnaw on them."

"Has he," said Hawkheel.

"I suppose you're going up there to look at them."

"Well," said Hawkheel, "I might."

The Stong place was high on a bluff, a mile upstream from Hawkheel's trailer as the crow flew. To Hawkheel, every turn of the road was like the bite of an auger into the past. He did not remember his adult journeys up Stong's driveway, but recalled with vivid clarity sitting in the dust-colored passenger seat of their old Ford while his father drove over a sodden mat of leaves. The car window had been cranked down, and far below, the hissing river, heavy with rain, cracked boulders along its bottom. His father drove jerkily, lips moving in whispered conversation with invisi-

❦ ❦ ❦

ble imps. Hawkheel had kept his hand on the door handle in case
the old man steered for the edge and he had to jump. It was one
of the last memories he had of his father.

The Stong place, he saw now, had run down. The real-estate
agents would get it pretty soon. The sagging clapboard house tapered away into a long ell and the barn. The store was still in the
ell, but Hawkheel took the old shortcut around back, driving
through the stinging nettles and just catching a glimpse through
the store window of Stong's white head bobbing over a handful
of papers.

The barn was filled with dim, brown light shot through like Indian silk with brilliant threads of sunlight. There was a faint
smell of apples. On the other side of the wall a rooster beat his
wings. Hawkheel looked around and saw, behind the grain sacks,
hundreds of books, some in boxes, some stacked on shelves and
windowsills. The first one he took up was a perfect copy of Thad
Norris's 1865 *The American Angler's Book*. He'd seen it listed in
his catalogue at home at $85. Stong wanted one dollar.

Hawkheel went at the boxes. He turned out Judge Nutting's
nice little book on grouse, *The History of One Day Out of Seven-
teen Thousand*. A box of stained magazines was hiding a rare
1886 copy of Halford's *Floating Flies,* the slipcase deeply
marked with Stong's penciled price of $1.50.

"Oh god," said Hawkheel, "I got him now."

He disguised the valuable books by mixing them with dull-
jacketed works on potatoes and surveying, and carried the stack
into the feed store. Stong sat at the counter, working his adding
machine. Hawkheel noticed he had taken to wearing overalls,
and a bandana knotted around his big neck. He looked to see if
there was a straw hat on a nail.

"Good to see you, Leverd," said Stong in a creamy voice. He
gossiped and joked as if Hawkheel were one of the summer people, winked and said, "Don't spend your whole social security
check on books, Leverd. Save a little out for a good time. You
seen the new Ruger shotguns?" A mellowed and ripened Stong,
improved by admiration, thought Hawkheel.

The books had belonged to Stong's grandfather, a hero of the waters whose name had once been in the Boston papers for his record trout. The stuffed and mounted trout still hung on the store wall beside the old man's enlarged photograph showing his tilted face and milky eyes behind the oval curve of glass.

"Bill, what will you take for your grandpa today?" cried the summer people who jammed the store on Saturdays, and Stong always answered, "Take what I can get," making a country virtue out of avarice.

Stong was ready to jump into his grandfather stories with a turn of the listener's eye. "The old fool was so slack-brained he got hisself killed with crow bait."

Hawkheel, coming in from the barn with book dust on him, saw that Stong still lied as easily as he breathed. The summer people stood around him like grinning dogs waiting for the warm hearts and livers of slain hares.

Stong's best customers were the autumn hunters. They re-opened their summer camps, free now from wives and children, burned the wood they had bought in August from Bucky Pincoke and let the bottle of bourbon stand out on the kitchen table with the deck of cards.

"Roughin' it, are you?" Stong would cry jovially to Mr. Rose, splendid in his new red L.L. Bean suspenders. The hunters bought Stong's knives and ammunition and went away with rusted traps, worn horseshoes and bent pokers pulled from the bins labeled "Collector's Items." In their game pockets were bottles of Stong's cheap Spanish wine, faded orange from standing in the sun. Stong filled their ears to overflowing with his inventions.

"Yes," he would say, "that's what Antler Mountain is named for, not because there's any big bucks up there, which there is *not*"—with a half wink for Hawkheel who stood in the doorway holding rare books like hot bricks—"but because this couple named Antler, Jane and Anton Antler, lived up there years ago. Kind of simple, like some old families hereabouts get."

A sly look. Did he mean Hawkheel's father, who was carted

away with wet chin and shaking hands to the state asylum believing pitchfork handles were adders?

"Yes, they had a little cabin up there. Lived off raccoons and weeds. Then old Jane had this baby, only one they ever had. Thought a lot of it, couldn't do enough for it, but it didn't survive their care and when it was only a few months old it died."

Stong, like a petulant tenor, turned away then and arranged the dimes in the cash register. The hunters rubbed their soft hands along the counter and begged for the rest of the story. Hawkheel himself wondered how it would come out.

"Well, sir, they couldn't bear to lay that baby away in the ground, so they put it in a five-gallon jar of pure alcohol. My own grandfather—used to stand right here behind the counter where I'm standing now—sold 'em the jar. We used to carry them big jars. Can't get 'em any more. They set that jar with the baby on a stump in front of their cabin the way we might set out a plaster duck on the lawn." He would pause a moment for good effect, then say, *"The stump's still there."*

They asked him to draw maps on the back of paper bags and went up onto the Antler to stare at the stump as if the impression of the jar had been burned into it by holy fire. Stong, with a laugh like a broken cream separator, told Hawkheel that every stick from that cut maple was in his woodshed. For each lie he heard, Hawkheel took three extra books.

All winter long Hawkheel kept digging away at the book mine in the barn, putting good ones at the bottom of the deepest pile so no one else would find them, cautiously buying only a few each week.

"Why, you're getting to be my best customer, Leverd," said Stong, looking through the narrow, handmade Dutch pages of John Beever's *Practical Fly-fishing,* which Hawkheel guessed was worth $200 on the collector's market, but for which Stong wanted only fifty cents. Hawkheel was afraid Stong would feel the quality of paper, notice that it was a numbered copy, somehow sense its rarity and value. He tried a diversion.

᭡᭡᭡

"Bill! You'll be interested that last week I seen the heaviest buck I seen in many years. He was pawing through the leaves about thirty yards from My Place."

In Chopping County "My Place" meant the speaker's private deer stand. It was a county of still hunting, and good stands were passed from father to son. Hawkheel's Place on the Antler regularly gave him big deer, usually the biggest deer in Feather River. Stong's old Place in the comfortable pine was useless, discovered by weekend hunters from out of state who shot his bucks and left beer cans under the tree while he tended the store. They brought the deer to be weighed on Stong's reporting scales, bragging, not knowing they'd usurped his stand, while he smiled and nodded. Stong had not even had a small doe in five years.

"Your Place up on the Antler, Leverd?" said Stong, letting the cover of the Beever fall closed. "Wasn't that over on the south slope?"

"No, it's in that beech stand on the shoulder. Too steep for flat-landers to climb so I do pretty good there. A big buck. I'd say he'd run close to one-eighty, dressed."

Stong raked the two quarters toward him and commenced a long lie about a herd of white deer that used to live in the swamp in the old days, but his eyes went back to the book in Hawkheel's hands.

The long fine fishing days began a few weeks later, and Hawkheel decided to walk the high northeast corner of the county looking for new water. In late summer he found it.

At the head of a rough mountain pass a waterfall poured into a large trout pool like champagne into a wine glass. Images of clouds and leaves lay on the slowly revolving surface. Dew, like crystal insect eggs, shone in the untrodden moss along the stream. The kingfisher screamed and clattered his wings as Hawkheel played a heavy rainbow into the shallows. In a few weeks he came to think that since the time of the St. Francis Indians, only he had ever found the way there.

As August waned Hawkheel grew possessive of the pool and arranged stones and twigs when he could not come for several days, searching later for signs of their disarray from trespassing feet. Nothing was ever changed, except when a cloudburst washed his twigs into a huddle.

One afternoon the wind came up too strong to cast from below the pool, and Hawkheel took off his shoes and stockings and crept cautiously onto the steep rock slab above the waterfall. He gripped his bare white toes into the granite fissures, climbing the rough face. The wind blew his hair up the wrong way and he felt he must look like the kingfisher.

From above the pool he could see the trout swimming smoothly in the direction of the current. The whole perspective of the place was new; it was as if he were seeing it for the first time. There was the back of the dead spruce and the kingfisher's hidden entrance revealed. There, too, swinging from an invisible length of line wound around a branch stub, was a faded red and white plastic bobber that the Indians had not left.

"Isn't anything safe any more?" shouted Hawkheel, coming across the rock too fast. He went down hard and heard his knee crack. He cursed the trout, the spruce, the rock, the invader of his private peace, and made a bad trip home leaning on a forked stick.

Urna brought over hot suppers until he could get around and do for himself again. The inside of the trailer was packed with books and furniture and the cramped space made him listless. He got in the habit of cooking only every three or four days, making up big pots of venison stew or pea soup and picking at it until it was used up or went bad.

He saw in the mirror that he looked old. He glared at his reflection and asked, "Where's your medicine bottle and sweater?" He thought of his mother who sat for years in the rocker, her thick, ginger-shellacked cane hooked over the arm, and fled into his books, reading until his eyes stung and his favorites were too familiar to open. The heavy autumnal rain hammered on the trailer and stripped the leaves from the trees. Not until the day before deer season was he well enough to drive up to Stong's feed store for more books.

He went through the familiar stacks gloomily, keeping his weight off the bad leg and hoping to find something he'd overlooked among the stacks of fine-printed agricultural reports and ink-stained geographies.

He picked up a big dark album that he'd passed over a dozen times. The old-fashioned leather cover was stamped with a design of flowing feathers in gold, and tortured gothic letters spelled "Family Album." Inside he saw photographs, snapshots, ocher newspaper clippings whose paste had disintegrated, postcards, prize ribbons. The snapshots showed scores of curd-faced Stongs squinting into the sun, Stong children with fat knees holding wooden pull-along ducks, and a black and white dog Hawkheel dimly remembered.

He looked closer at one snapshot, drawn by something familiar. A heavy boy stood on a slab of rock, grinning up into the sky. In his hand a fishing rod pointed at the upper branches of a spruce where a bobber was hopelessly entangled in the dark needles. A blur of moving water rushed past the boy into a black pool.

"You bastard," said Hawkheel, closing the album on the picture of Stong, Bill Stong of years ago, trespassing at Hawkheel's secret pool.

He pushed the album up under the back of his shirt so it lay against his skin. It felt the size of a Sears' catalogue and made him throw out his shoulders stiffly. He took a musty book at random—*The Boy's Companion*—and went out to the treacherous Stong.

"Haven't seen you for quite a while, Leverd. Hear you been laid up," said Stong.

"Bruised my knee." Hawkheel put the book on the counter.

"Got to expect to be laid up now and then at our age," said Stong. "I had trouble with my hip off and on since April. I got something here that'll fix you up." He took a squat, foreign bottle out from under the counter.

"Mr. Rose give me this for checking his place last winter. Apple brandy, and about as strong as anything you ever tasted. Too strong for me, Leverd. I get dizzy just smelling the cork." He poured a little into a paper cup and pushed it at Hawkheel.

The fragrance of apple wood and autumn spread out as Hawkheel tasted the Calvados. A column of fire rose in the chimney of his throat with a bitter aftertaste like old cigar smoke.

"I suppose you're all ready for opening day, Leverd. Where you going for deer this year?"

"Same place I always go—My Place up on the Antler."

"You been up there lately?"

"No, not since spring." Hawkheel felt the album's feathered design transferring to his back.

"Well, Leverd," said Stong in a mournful voice, "there's no deer up there now. Got some people bought land up there this summer, think the end of the world is coming so they built a cement cabin, got in a ton of dried apricots and pinto beans. They got some terrible weapons to keep the crowds away. Shot up half the trees on the Antler testing their machine guns. Surprised you didn't hear it. No deer within ten miles of the Antler now. You might want to try someplace else. They say it's good over to Slab City."

Hawkheel knew one of Stong's lies when he heard it and wondered what it meant. He wanted to get home with the album and examine the proof of Stong's trespass at the secret pool, but Stong poured from the bottle again and Hawkheel knocked it back.

"Where does your fancy friend get this stuff?" he asked, feeling electrical impulses sweep through his fingers as though they itched to play the piano.

"Frawnce," said Stong in an elegant tone. "He goes there every year to talk about books at some college." His hard eyes glittered with malice. "He's a liberian." Stong's thick forefinger opened the cover of *The Boy's Companion,* exposing a red-bordered label Hawkheel had missed; it was marked $55.

"He says I been getting skinned over my books, Leverd."

"Must of been quite a shock to you," said Hawkheel, thinking he didn't like the taste of apple brandy, didn't like librarian Rose. He left the inflated *Boy's Companion* on the counter and hobbled out to the truck, the photograph album between his shoulder blades giving him a ramrod dignity. In the rearview mirror he saw Stong at the door staring after him.

Clouds like grey waterweed under the ice choked the sky and a gusting wind banged the door against the trailer. Inside, Hawkheel worked the album out from under his shirt and laid it on the table while he built up the fire and put on some leftover pea soup to heat. " 'Liberian!' " he said once and snorted. After supper he felt queasy and went to bed early thinking the pea soup might have stood too long.

In the morning Hawkheel's bowels beat with urgent tides of distress and there was a foul taste in his mouth. When he came back from the bathroom he gripped the edge of the table which bent and surged in his hands, then gave up and took to his bed. He could hear sounds like distant popcorn and thought it was knotty wood in the stove until he remembered it was the first day of deer season. "Goddammit," he cried, "I already been stuck here six weeks and now I'm doing it again."

A sound woke him in late afternoon. He was thirsty enough to drink tepid water from the spout of the teakettle. There was another shot on the Antler and he peered out the window at the shoulder of the mountain. He thought he could see specks of brightness in the dull grey smear of hardwood and brush, and he shuffled over to the gun rack to get his .30-.30, clinging to the backs of the chairs for balance. He rested the barrel on the breadbox and looked through the scope, scanning the slope for his deer stand, and at once caught the flash of orange.

He could see two of them kneeling beside the bark-colored curve of a dead deer at his Place. He could make out the bandana at the big one's neck, see a knife gleam briefly like falling water. He watched them drag the buck down toward the logging road until the light faded and their orange vests turned black under the trees.

"Made sure I couldn't go out with your goddamned poison brandy, didn't you?" said Hawkheel.

He sat by the stove with the old red Indian blanket pulled around him, feeling like he'd stared at a light bulb too long. Urna called after supper. Her metallic voice rang in his ear.

"I suppose you heard all about it."

"Only thing I heard was the shots, but I seen him through the scope from the window. What'd it weigh out at?"

"I heard two-thirty, dressed out, so live weight must of been towards three hundred. Warden said it's probably the biggest buck ever took in the county, a sixteen-pointer, too, and probably a state record. I didn't know you could see onto the Antler from your window."

"Oh, I can see good, but not good enough to see who was with him."

"He's the one bought Willard Iron's place and put a tennis court onto the garden," said Urna scornfully. "Rose. They say he was worse than Bill, jumping around and screaming for them to take pictures."

"Did they?"

"Course they did. Then they all went up to Mr. Tennis Court's to have a party. Stick your head out the door and you'll hear them on the wind."

Hawkheel did not stick his head out the door, but opened the album to look at the Stongs, their big, rocklike faces bent over wedding cakes and infants. Many of the photographs were captioned in a spiky, antique hand: "Cousin Mattie with her new skates," "Pa on the porch swing," simple statements of what was already clear as though the writer feared the images would someday dissolve into blankness, leaving the happiness of the Stongs unknown.

He glared, seeing Stong at the secret pool, the familiar sly eyes, the fatuous gaping mouth unchanged. He turned the pages to a stiff portrait of Stong's parents, the grandfather standing behind them holding what Hawkheel thought was a cat until he recognized the stuffed trout. On the funeral page the same portraits were reduced in size and joined by a flowing black ribbon that bent and curled in ornate flourishes. The obituary from the *Rutland Herald* was headlined "A Farm Tragedy."

"Too bad Bill missed that dinner," said Hawkheel.

He saw that on many pages there were empty places where photographs had been wrenched away. He found them, mutilated and torn, at the end of the album. Stong was in every photograph. In the high school graduation picture, surrounded by clouds of organdy and stiff new suits, Stong's face was inked out and black blood ran from the bottoms of his trousers. Here was another, Stong on a fat-tired white bicycle with a dozen arrows drawn piercing his body. A self-composed obituary, written in a hand like infernal corrosive lace that scorched the page, told how this miserable boy, "too bad to live" and "hated by everybody" had met his various ends. Over and over Stong had killed his photographic images. He listed every member of his family as a survivor.

Hawkheel was up and about the next morning, a little unsteady but with a clear head. At first light the shots had begun on the Antler, hunters trying for a buck to match the giant that Stong had brought down. The Antler, thought Hawkheel, was as good as bulldozed.

By afternoon he felt well enough for a few chores, stacking hay bales around the trailer foundation and covering the windows over with plastic. He took two trout out of the freezer and fried them for supper. He was washing the frying pan when Urna called.

"They was on T.V. with the deer," she said. "They showed the game commissioner looking up the record in some book and saying this one beat it. I been half expecting to hear from you all day, wondering what you're going to do."

"Don't you worry," said Hawkheel. "Bill's got it comin' from me. There's a hundred things I could do."

✵✵✵

"Well," said Urna, "he's got it coming."

It took Hawkheel forty minutes to pack the boxes and load them into the pickup. The truck started hard after sitting in the cold blowing rain for two days, but by the time he got it onto the main road it ran smooth and steady, the headlights opening a sharp yellow path through the night.

At the top of Stong's drive he switched the lights off and coasted along in neutral. A half-full moon, ragged with rushing clouds, floated in the sky. Another storm breeder, thought Hawkheel.

The buck hung from a gambrel in the big maple, swaying slowly in the gusting wind. The body cavity gaped black in the moonlight. "Big," said Hawkheel, seeing the glint of light on the hooves scraping an arc in the leaves, "damn big." He got out of the truck and leaned his forehead against the cold metal for a minute.

From a box in the back of the truck he took one of his books and opened it. It was *Haw-Ho-Noo*. He leaned over a page as if he could read the faint print in the moonlight, then gripped it and tore it out. One after another he seized the books, ripped the pages and cracked their spines. He hurled them at the black, swaying deer and they fell to the bloodied ground beneath it.

"Fool with me, will you?" shouted Hawkheel, tearing soft paper with both hands, tossing books up at the moon, and his blaring sob rose over the sound of the boulders cracking in the river below.

Stone City

THE dark-colored fox trotted along the field edge with his nose down, following the woodsline of his property—his by right of use. His smoky pelt was still dull from molting and had not yet begun to take on its winter lustre. A stalk of panic grass shivered and he pounced, then crunched the grasshopper.

He skirted the silver ruins of abandoned farm buildings and spent some time in the orchard eating windfalls. Then he left the apple trees, crossed the brook at the back of the field, pausing to lap the water, and moved into the woods. He went familiarly into the poplars, black ears pricked to the turn of a leaf, nose taking up the rich streams of scent that flowed into the larger river of rotted leaf mold and earth.

1

At the time I moved into Chopping County, Banger was about fifty, a heavy man, all suet and mouth. At first I thought he was that stock character who remembered everybody's first name, shouting "Har ya! How the hell ya doin'?" to people he'd seen only an hour before, giving them a slap on the back or a punch on the arm—swaggering gestures in school, but obnoxious in a middle-aged man. I saw him downtown, talking to anybody who would listen, while he left his hardware store to the attentions of a slouchy kid who could never find anything on the jumbled shelves.

I made the mistake of saying what I thought about Banger one night at the Bear Trap Grill. The bar was a slab of varnished pine; the atmosphere came from a plastic moose on top of the cash register and a mason jar half-filled with pennies.

I wanted to find somebody to go bird shooting with, somebody who knew the good coverts in the slash-littered mountainous country. I'd always hunted alone, self-taught, doing what I guessed was right, but still believing that companionship increased the pleasure of hunting, just as "layin' up" with somebody, as they said locally, was better than sleeping alone.

I was sitting next to Tukey. His liver-spotted hands shook; hard to get a straight answer from him or anyone else. They said he was a pretty good man for grouse. They said he might take company. I'd been courting him, hoping for an invitation to go out when the season opened. I thought I had him ready to say, "Hell yes, come on along."

Banger was at the end of the bar talking nonstop to deaf Fance who had hearing-aid switches all over the front of his shirt. Tukey said Fance had a gun collection in his spare bedroom and was afraid to sleep at night, afraid thieves would break in when the hearing aids lay disconnected on the bedside table.

"God, that Banger. He's always here, always yapping. Doesn't he ever go home?" I asked Tukey. In ten seconds I scratched weeks of softening the old man up. All that beer for nothing. His face pleated like a closing concertina.

"Well, now, as a matter of fact, he don't, much. His place burned down and the wife and kid was fried right up in it. He got nothing left but his dog and the goddamn hardware store his old man left him and which he was never suited to.

"And my advice to you," Tukey said, "if you want to go out bird shootin' like you been hintin' around, or deer or 'coon or rabbit or bear huntin', or," and his dried-leaf voice rose to a mincing falsetto, "just enjoyin' the rare beauties of our woodlands . . ." He broke off to grin maliciously, exposing flawless plastic teeth, to let me know they had seen me walking in the woods with neither rod nor gun in my hands.

His voice dropped again, weighted with sarcasm. "My advice

to you if you want to know where the birds is, is to get real friendly with that Banger you think is so tiresome. What he don't know about this country is less than *that*." He raised the dirty stub of an amputated forefinger, the local badge of maimedness that set those who worked with chain saws apart from lesser men.

"Him?" I glanced at Banger punctuating his torrent of words with intricate gestures. He pointed with his chin and his hands flew up into the air like birds.

"Yes, him. And if you go huntin' with him I'd like to hear about it, because Banger keeps to himself. Nobody, not me, not Fance, has went out huntin' with him for years." He turned away from me. I finished my drink and left. There was nothing else to do.

I didn't bother with the locals again, except Noreen Pineaud: thirties, russet hair, powder-blue stretch pants and golden eyes in a sharp little fox face. On Fridays she cleaned the house.

She stayed for a cup of coffee and smoked a cigarette one Friday, after I wrote her check. We sat at the kitchen table. She told me she was separated from her husband. That old question hung there. The check lay on the table between us.

I didn't say anything, I didn't move, and after a minute she tapped out the cigarette in the aluminum frozen-pie pan that was all I could find for an ashtray. She did it gently to show there weren't any hard feelings.

I had retreated from other people in other places like a man backing fearfully out of a quicksand bog he has stumbled into unknowingly. This place in Chopping County was my retreat from high, muddy water.

Noreen looked a lot like the kid in Banger's hardware store. I asked her.

"Yeah, he's one of my nephews, Raymie. My brother, Raymon', he don't want the kid to work for Banger. He's real strict, Raymon'. Says it's a fag job. See, he wants the kid to trap or get a job cuttin' wood." She turned her sharp face to follow the trail of drifting headlights outside the window.

"Raymon' made a lot of money with a trapline when he was a kid, and now the prices for furs are real good again. Foxes and stuff. So he got Raymie these twenty-five traps a coupla weeks ago. Now he says Raymie's gotta set 'em out and run the trapline before he goes down to the hardware store in the mornin'. You know how long that takes? Raymie takes after his mother. He like things easy."

She talked on, uncoiling intricate ropes of blood relationship, telling me who was married to whom, the favorite small-town subject. I listened, out of the swamp now and onto dry ground.

That fall I went alone for the birds as I always had. No dog, alone, and with my mother's gun, a .28-gauge Parker. Thank you kindly, ma'am, it's the only thing you ever gave me except a strong inclination toward mistrust. She wrote her own epitaph, a true doubter to the last.

> *Although I sleep in dust awhile*
> *Beneath the barren clod,*
> *Ere long I hope to rise and smile*
> *To meet my Saviour God*
> *If He exists.*

The first morning of the season was cold, the frosted clumps of tussock grass like spiral nebulae. I went up the hardwood slopes, the trees growing out of a cascade of shattered rock spilled by the last glacier. No birds in this grey monotony of beech and maple, and I kept climbing for the ridges where stands of spruce knotted dark shelter in their branches.

The slope leveled off; in a rain-filled hollow a rind of ice imprisoned the leaves, soot-black, brown, umber, grey-tan like the coats of deer, in its glassy clasp. No birds.

I walked up into the conifers, my panting the only sound. Fox tracks in the hoarfrost. The weight of the somber sky pressed down with the heaviness of a coming storm. No birds in the spruce. Under the trees the hollows between the roots were bowls filled with ice crystals like moth antennae. The birds were somewhere else, close hugging other trees while they waited for the foul weather to hit, or even now above me, rigidly stretched out to imitate broken branch stubs in the web of interlacing conifers, invisible and silent, watching the fool who wandered below, a passing hat and a useless tube of steel tied to the ground by earth's inertia.

What, I thought, like every grouse hunter has thought, what if I could fly, could glide through the spruce leaders and smile down into the smug, feathery faces like an old ogre confronting the darling princess. The view from the ground was green bottlebrushes, impenetrable, confusing, secretive, against a sky the color of an old galvanized pail. No birds.

The dull afternoon smothered a faraway shotgun blast from some distant ridge, quickly followed by another. He missed the first time, I thought. It was less a sound than a feeling in the bone, muted strokes like a maul driving fence posts. I wondered if it were Banger. Banger would not have missed the first shot. It must have been a double.

Even now, as I stood listening to the locked silence, he was probably taking the second bird from his dog's mouth, fanning the tail, smoothing down the broken feathers and opening the crop to see the torn leaves of mitrewort and wood sorrel spill out. I could imagine him talking to the dog, to the fallen bird, to his shotgun. I felt an affinity to that distant grouse hunter that I could never feel for the downtown talker.

In the weeks that followed I often hunted that ridge where the beech spread into the spruce like outstretched fingers. I heard the increasingly familiar shotgun from the second ridge beyond mine. I put up birds and I took some down.

Too many times I had to crawl on hands and knees through slash where a wounded bird had dropped, praying it hadn't crept into a stump where I could never find it, where it would die. One I did lose. Five hours of beating back and forth in a swamp, poking into rotted logs, kicking heaps of slash and damning the lack of a dog and my atrophied sense of smell. Again that maul stroke from the second ridge, a single shot, and I envied Banger his dog. I had to leave my bird unfound.

The loss of the bird spoiled that place for me, and I decided to work over to the lean spine of rock where Banger and his dog hunted. I was sure by now that my distant hunting companion was Banger, mythical friend, sprung from the echoes of a firing mechanism, the unknown Banger imprisoned in the loudmouth's shell.

The first early snows came and melted and we were into Indian summer. The sky was an intense enamel blue, but the afternoon light had a dying, year's-end quality, a rich apricot color as though it fell through a cordial glass onto an oak table, the kind of day hunters remember falsely as October.

It was a day for birds. They would be lounging in favorite dust bowls, feeding languidly on thorn apples like oriental princes sucking sugared dates. A late patch of jewelweed with a few ragged blossoms in a wet swale caught my eye halfway up the ridge. There was a thick stand of balsam at the far end. The jewelweed had a picked-over look, and the balsams had good ground openings for walking birds. It felt birdy.

I breathed shallowly to keep my heartbeat from vibrating the air. I knew the birds saw me, knew that I knew they were there, and I waited for the wave of adrenaline to pass, for the hot blows of blood to subside. I slid the safety off.

The birds were invisible in the runways under the firs, resting after a morning of snapping off the jewelweed flowers that burst halfway down their throats. Young birds, I thought, into the jewelweed. They would fly up as soon as I took a step forward.

I stayed still, never quite ready, the moment taking me. I waited too long, and a delicate pattering in the leaves of the hardwoods beyond the balsams like the first tentative drops of rain told me the birds had walked away, young tender grouse with pinkish breastbones who might have been flushed, might still be flushed, but who had won this particular encounter. Let them have the jewelweed and the October sunlight this time.

I skirted the balsam stand and came out on the back of Banger's ridge. When I looked down I saw Stone City.

There are some places that fill us with immediate loathing and fear. A friend once described to me a circle of oaks behind a farmhouse in Iowa that made the hair on the back of his neck stand up. Later he heard that the body of a murdered child had been found there, half-covered with wet soil, a decade earlier. I felt something evil tincturing the pale light that washed my first view of Stone City.

It was an abandoned farm lying between two ridges, no roads in or out, only a faint track choked with viburnum and alder. The property, shaped like an eye, was bordered on the back by a stream. Popple and spruce had invaded the hayfields, and the broken limbs of the apple trees hung to the ground.

The buildings were gone, collapsed into cellar holes of rotting beams. Blackberry brambles boiled out of the crumbling foundations and across a fallen blue door that half-blocked a cellar hole.

I came cautiously down the slope to the fields. The grass hummed with cicadas, crickets and grasshoppers that had escaped the early frosts. The buzzing stopped as I stepped into the field. The soil looked thin. A long backbone of rock jutted from the pasture. Something of the vanished owner's grim labor showed in a curious fenceline that would stand another hundred years; the fence "posts" were old iron wagon axles sunk deep into holes hand drilled in the granite ledge.

There was no wind. Yellowjackets were at the rotten apples under the orchard trees. The light fell slow, heavy. Inhaling the sharp odor of acetic, rotted fruit I stepped into the honey-colored field. I remembered the feeling I had as a child, of sadness in the early fall.

A bird tore from the apple tree with a sound like ripping silk straight toward the narrow neck of field that closed into trees. Feathers made a brief aerial fountain and I marked the bird's fall into quivering grass as I dropped the gun. A second, a third and a fourth roar, the air was full of birds, breakers of sound over my head, bird flight and shotgun beating against the walls of hillside and birds falling like fruits, hitting the ground with ripe thumps. Only the first of them was mine.

A bell tinkled and a Brittany came into the field to pick them up. Banger said, "You stepped out just the same time as I did. You the one I hear shootin' up in the Choppin' Swamp these past weeks?" He didn't look at me. The dog brought all the birds to Banger.

"Nice shooting," I said. The birds were good-sized. "What is this place?" There were three hens and a smaller cock.

Banger looked around and twisted up his mouth a little. He took up a bird and gutted it.

"This place, this old farm, is a place I used to hunt when I was a kid. I was run offa here three times, and the last time I was helped along with number six birdshot. Still got the little pick scars all acrost my back. Old man Stone. Shot me when I was a kid, tryin' to run me off." He pulled the viscera of the second bird from the hot cavity.

"Place used to be called Stone City. I still call it that. Stone City. The Stones all lived up here—three or four different families of them. Their own little city. Tax collector never come up here. No game warden, nobody except me, a kid after the birds. There's always been birds here."

"What happened to the Stones?"

"Oh, they just died out and moved away." His voice trailed off. I didn't know then he was lying.

The afternoon sun streamed over Banger's dog who sat close to his leg. His hand went out and cupped her bony skull. "My dog," he said. "All I got in the world, ain'tcha, Lady?"

He squatted on the ground and looked into the dog's eyes. I was embarrassed by their intimacy, by the banal name, "Lady," by the self-pity in Banger's voice. No, I thought, there was no way

I could be Banger's hunting companion. He had his dog. So it was a shock when the dog walked over to me and licked my hand.

"My Jesus," said Banger. "She never done that in her life."

He didn't like it.

We walked back past the cellar holes toward the spruce at the end of the fields. Banger's dog walked beside and one step behind him.

"Give you a ride," said Banger.

His old Power Wagon was parked on a logging road half a mile below Stone City. It rode rough, bottoming out on hummocks and rocks. Lady sat in the middle and stared straight ahead like a dowager being driven to the opera. Banger shouted at me over the roar and clatter of the truck.

"Old man Stone . . . meanest bastard I ever . . . all his sons and daughters wilder . . . mean . . . and they was a lot of them." The gears crashed and Banger wheeled the truck onto the main road.

"They had all these little shacks with broken-down rusty cars out front, piles of lumber and empty longnecks and pieces of machinery that might come in handy sometime, the weeds growin' up all crazy through 'em everywhere. The Stone boys was all wild, jacked deer, trapped bear, dynamited trout pools, made snares, shot strange dogs wasn't their own and knocked up every girl they could put it to. Yessir, they was some bunch." He turned onto a dirt road that ended at the sugarhouse he'd fixed up.

"Should of looked at what I was doin'. Guess I brought you home with me, I'm so used to turnin' up the hill. Fried bird for supper. You might as well stay."

He took down four birds from the side of his woodshed and hung up those in his game vest. He wouldn't let me help pluck the supper birds but waved me into the sugarhouse. Lady raced around him, chasing the down feathers in the rising late afternoon wind.

I looked around inside. There were a few books on a shelf, some pots and pans hanging from nails, the dog's dish and a braided Discount Mart rug behind the stove. Banger's cot, narrow as a plank, stood against the far wall. I thought of him lying in it, night after night, listening to the dog's snuffling dreams behind the stove.

The place was something of a grouse museum with spread pat tails mounted on the walls—greys, a few cinnamon reds and one rare lemon-yellow albino. Curled snapshots of Banger as a young man with grouse in his hands were stapled up beside colored pages cut from hunting magazines, showing grouse on the wing. There were shotguns hanging from pegs and propped in the corners. A badly mounted grouse of great size, tilted a little to one side as though it were fainting, stood on a section of log behind the door, and nests of dried-up grouse eggs on a little shelf must have dated back to Banger's boyhood collecting days, featherlight shells filled with dried scraps of embryonic grouse.

I lit the kerosene lamp on the table, illuminating a framed photograph in a wreath of plastic flowers, a picture of a girl standing in front of a farmhouse with a sagging roof. She had long hair, the ends blurred as though the wind were blowing it when the shutter snapped. She squinted into the sunlight, holding a clump of daisies hastily snatched up at the last minute for effect. I could see the clot of soil clinging to the roots. Banger's dead wife.

Lard spattered out of the frying pan and flared, ticks of flame, as Banger dropped in the floury pieces of grouse. He sprinkled salt and pepper, then threw the fresh livers and giblets of the day's bag to Lady behind the stove.

We ate in silence. Banger's jaws worked busily on the savory birds. He said nothing for a change. The oil lamp flame crept higher. I thought of wagon axles set in granite ledge and asked what old Stone was like.

"He was the worst of the whole goddamn tribe. Had kids that was his grandkids. Dirty old tyrant, used to whip 'em all, keep 'em in fear." His fingers drummed a partridge roll on the table. He shouted at the photograph of the girl, continuing an unfinished argument. "The old pig ought to have had nails pounded into his eyes and a blunt fence post hammered up his asshole!" Banger's voice choked.

I did not see him for nearly a month after that dinner.

2

The dark fox trotted behind the screen of chokecherries along the highway, undisturbed by the swishing roar of vehicles twenty feet away. This was the extreme southern border of his range and he never crossed this road. The corpse of a less-wise raven lay beneath a bush like a patch of melted tar. The fox rolled in the carrion, grinding his shoulders into it. He got up, shook himself and continued his tour, a black feather in the fur of his shoulder like a dart placed by a picador.

As swiftly as though she were pulling grass Noreen plucked the second bird. The other lay on the white enamel drainboard, a dusky purple color.

"Oh, I don't mind doin' it. I done hundreds of 'em. There was one or two years when I was a kid, things were real bad up here, no jobs, no money. We lived on pats and fish—trout, suckers, anything. I used to clean the birds." Her fingers leaped from the small body in her left hand to the pile of feathers in the sink and back again.

"My brother Raymon' done the fish. He never liked the smell of a bird's guts, but it don't bother me. He can skin out or clean any other kind of animal just as fast and good, but not birds. I don't mind 'em."

There were five or six dull *pocks* as she yanked the difficult wing tip feathers. "Okay, there you are." They lay side by side, dark cavities between their rigidly upthrust legs. Noreen leaned against the sink, dove-grey twilight washing up around her like rising water. Her russet hair was twisted into curls and there was a downy feather on her cheek. She sang a few words that sounded like "won't lay down with Cowboy Joe." The hell with Cowboy Joe, I thought, what about me?

It wasn't the first time I've been in a bed that turned into a confessional afterwards.

"You married?"

"Yes."

"Yeah, me too. I knew you were." The vixen face was pale in the thickening dusk.

"My brother," she said. "My brother Raymon', you know?"

"Yes."

"He ain't my full brother, see, he's only my half brother." Her voice was a child's, telling secrets. "See, Ma had him before she met my dad, and Dad give him his name." The bed was a fox's den, rank fox smell, the smell of earth. She whispered. "I done it with Raymon'."

"When?"

"Long ago, the first time, see? He's only my half brother. That was the only time." She looked at me. "Now you."

"Now me what?"

"Now you got to tell something bad you done."

It stopped being a game. Unbidden, to my mind came childhood crimes and adult cruelties. I was furious to feel prickling tears.

"Tell me about Raymond," I said.

"See, she was goin' with this guy, he come from a family that used to live around here—the Stones, they don't live here now—and Raymon' was on the way, but before they could get married there was some bad trouble so Raymon' didn't have a father. It was real love and she almost went crazy. But she met my father, he was cuttin' wood over here, workin' for St. Regis. He come from a town up in Quebec."

"So Raymond is really a Stone?"

"Yeah. Well, he never used the name, but that's his blood. That's half his blood."

I thought of Stone City, the broken shacks, the blue door with its peeling paint, the iron axles, the outlaw hideout.

"Which one of the Stones was he?" thinking of what Banger said about the old man.

She got up and began to dress in the faded evening. She smoothed back her hair with both hands. "This is between you and I," she whispered solemnly. "Floyd. He was the one that got the electric chair."

It became a regular thing. Every Friday night was confession night. I heard who killed the kitten, who stole a coveted blouse from a girlfriend. She was absorbed in family relationships. Most of all I heard about young Raymie's troubles with his old man, Raymon' the Half-Stone, as I thought of him.

"Raymie got another beatin' last night. See, he's got to run that trapline every twenty-four hours, and he's suppose to do it real early in the mornin' before he goes down to the hardware. Well, he forgot and you shoulda heard the way Raymon' tore that kid up. He's got a real violent temper. Raymie, he hates trappin'. He wants to get out of here, go to New York, be a rock singer. You ought to hear him."

3

There were only a few weeks left in the season. I did not let my new interest in the confessional break the pattern of birds. I went out every few days, sometimes only for an hour, sometimes until the end of the light. I did not go to Stone City, tinged with Banger's dark and private hatred. The first staying snows fell; the air hardened and crystallized to winter temper.

One morning, with the damp smell of coming snow hollowing my nostrils, I found Banger's and Lady's fresh tracks in the strip of hardwoods behind my house, bearing south. I took the deliberate trail as an invitation, thinking that perhaps it was the closest Banger could get to asking me to come along.

He had a good start. It was past noon by the time I reached Stone City. I'd traveled parallel to Banger's trail, but higher up the mountainside, thinking his earlier passage would have sent the birds sweeping and scuttling up the slope into hiding from storm and man.

I did well, flushing half a dozen in my slow hunt, for it was not a day when the birds moved easily. I brought one down, a reflex shot through a thick stand of young fir, as thin and crowded as bamboo, despite my cold-numbed thumb that could barely nudge the safety off. It grew increasingly colder and the snow began, serious snow.

Stone City was a desolate ruin, but Banger had a fire going in the shelter of a crumbled stone foundation wall and was boiling coffee in a small pot. The blue door was covered with snow. The flakes spit as they hit the flames. Banger threw on another silvered board from the collapsed house.

"Get anything?"

I held up the bird and described the shot. Banger spread the tail into a lady's fan, counted the feathers, flicking the two unbarred ones, gave me a look of reproach when he saw I had not opened the crop, and did so himself.

"Beechnuts. All mornin' they been gettin' 'em before the snow covers 'em all up. Every one a these"—he pointed at the four birds lying in a neat row—"was full up with beechnuts. Beechnut birds has got the best flavor."

I had never gotten the limit of birds in my life.

The coffee was hot and good. Banger said he always carried a little bag of coffee and the small pot in his game vest for the cold days. The fire burned down fast into plank-shaped coals. Banger went down into the cellar hole, looking for dry boards. He came out rubbing something on his sleeve.

"By god, look what I found on the top of the wall down there." He held it out to me. "That's old man Stone's knife."

It was a big folding knife with two blades, corroded, rusted. The body of the knife was a mottled yellow celluloid. There were shadowy images under the celluloid, flakes of images that suggested a pirate playing a concertina or a pile of books tumbling from a table while a mad professor grinned. There was a clearer image on the other side. A naked girl sat cross-legged on a beach, looking at the camera with a curved smile like the rim of a wineglass. Her hands patted a cone of sand between her legs.

I handed the knife back to Banger. It was heavy, as though it had gathered weight with age. Banger kept playing with it, trying to make out the shattered image. "By god, old man Stone's knife!" He laughed.

"What's the story on the Stone that was electrocuted?" I asked. Noreen had never gone back to the subject and a mutual delicacy kept either one of us from returning to that first conversation.

"Electrocuted? How'd you hear about that?"

I didn't answer and he turned the knife in his hands.

"That was Floyd Stone, the one that brought the whole pack of Stones down. He was a wild one, but not so wild as some of the others." The fresh planks smoked and then caught, blue flames rose elegantly along the edge of the boards. Lady put her head on Banger's knee and looked across the fire at me.

"How's my girl? How's my good old girl?" I said in that foolish voice I use with dogs I like. She wagged her feathery tail. Banger tightened his arm around her and I had a guilty rush as though I'd been caught caressing another man's wife.

"Floyd Stone. People around here had trouble with the Stones since the town began. Fact, the Stones were the first settlers here, but nobody brags about it.

"They come up from New Hampshire or down from Quebec, one, I don't know which. A real old family, and a real bad family. Floyd was just like all his brothers and cousins, had a crazy streak in him when he was drunk; he'd do anything, just anything. Always had a deer rifle with 'em, all of 'em.

"This one time he was drivin' up the hill from town, drunker'n a skunk, real hot, but not so loaded he couldn't navigate that old truck. Gets to the train crossin', train's goin' through. Seventy-three boxcars. He counts 'em. Two automobiles come up behind him, one the Baptist minister. End of the train comes. There's that guy standin' out on the little caboose porch. He waves to Floyd like them fellows do.

"Floyd picks up his .30–.30 quick as a snake and shoots the guy right through the head just like you or me woulda waved back. Shot him dead for no reason. Never even saw him before. Then he took off for up here. Stone City."

Banger pried a rusted blade out of the knife's body. "They come up to get him from all over. Had the state police, the sheriff, couple hundred men from down below, all had guns and anxious to use 'em. It was an army. The crowd was real ugly, had enough of Stones.

"Old man Stone come out on the porch. 'Git off my property!' he yells like he had a shotgun in his hands. But he didn't have no shotgun. Guess he would have if he hadn't been boiled himself. Holdin' a pitcher, one of them old tin pitchers, sloppin' full of some kind of homemade jungle juice. Just stood there, swayin' back and forth, eyes all red, yellin' 'Git off a my property!'

"State police yells back, 'We have a warrant here for the arrest of Floyd Stone for the willful murder of whoever he was, and so forth. Come on out, Floyd!'

"Course Floyd didn't come out. There was four or five houses here, could of been in any one of 'em, could of been in the woods. Then the state police says something to four of his guys and they run right up those porch steps and grab old man Stone and arrest him for obstructing justice. Right there was the porch." Banger pointed at the blue door.

"Fight, kick, scream, seventy years old, but that old man flashed out with his long fingernails and cut one of the state police right across the eyeball, fellow lost his eye and had to be pensioned off on full disability.

"Nobody wanted to go into them houses to look for Floyd. This was before they had mace and stuff that they squirt under doors. Crowd's ready for action, real savage. Somebody yells, 'Tear them houses down! That'll uncover the murderin' little prick!' Like I said, there was a couple hundred people there.

"They swarm all over those houses, pullin' rotten boards, kickin' in windows. Somebody got a axe and pried up the ends of the clapboards and ten more would rip it off like it was paper. Stones come flyin' out of those houses, women, kids, drunk Stones, some old granny, all of 'em yellin' and cryin'.

"Well, they got Floyd, too, in about ten minutes. He was layin' under the bed, hidin', had his old killer deer rifle under there with him, pointin' it at the bedroom door. He wasn't expectin' to have the whole back wall ripped off real sudden and a dozen guys grab his ankles and yank him out from under that bed. Police took him away—had some trouble to git him away, too—and left the rest of the Stones there with us. Somebody found some roofin' tar and started gettin' it hot."

I wondered if Banger had been the one to find the tar.

"They killed all the chickens for the feathers and some geese and ducks too. Then they stripped every one of them Stones except the women and the kids, and they poured that hot old tar right to 'em, went for the privates, and then they dumped on the feathers."

The snow drifted and whirled in the rising wind like down, like the flying feathers tossed onto the tarred Stones. A snow devil twisted briefly near the fallen porch. Christ, I thought, what kind of people were these?

4

Because of his color the fox rarely crossed open ground in snowy weather, but kept to woods and brush, mouse-hunting on the margins of open land. In the bitter dawn, his muzzle frosted, he headed for a bramble patch at the edge of a deserted field, hoping for a morning hare. Hare tracks ran like cats' cradles of tangled string, looping through the briars and into the spruce, then fading to nothing in the drifts as though the hare had unfolded strange wings and flown into the trees. Nose down, the fox trotted along, hoping for the warm scent, but there was only an elusive suggestion of hareishness. He was almost on the frozen shape in the snow before he caught the hateful odor of his greatest enemy. At almost the same time he was aware of the fact of death. His heart thudded, and so great was his agitation that he ran across an open meadow, an easy target for a fox hunter, had there been one.

During the night it turned intensely cold. A gusting wind rattled the windows and drove snow under the door. By Friday morning the snow had stopped but the wind scoured the ground bare in front of the house and built a knife-edged crescent drift across the drive.

A melancholy inertia, one of the ancient seven deadly sins, took me when Noreen called to say she would not come that day, that her car wouldn't start. Her voice rushed through the receiver, breathless and guilty. I wondered who she was with, maybe that husband whose name she had never mentioned, whose faults she had never described. Maybe her furious half brother, tainted with the rage of the Stones. There was a sense of mockery, the image of a curving smile and feathers flying in the wind.

I opened the oven door of the kitchen range for warmth and treated myself to a number of steaming toddies. The wind shook the stovepipe. I was alone, the glass was always empty. I dozed in the stifling kitchen, my head ringing with whiskey and the sound of the circling wind.

Banger stood in front of me, the kitchen door open, the wind cutting a corridor through the hot room. His bare hands were bent stiffly and his eyes streamed.

"Lady," he shouted. "You've got her, damn you. Where's my dog?"

We had to go through the house from attic to cellar, opening every closet and cupboard door before Banger believed that I didn't have Lady tied to a hidden water pipe. Noreen's blue slippers, shiny imitation satin with feathers, gleamed on the floor of the bedroom closet. I gave Banger a drink and listened.

He had let Lady out the night before despite the snow, he said, snuffling and wiping his nose on the back of his hand. Lady enjoyed an hour or so out on bad nights. He thought she liked it because it made the warm spot behind the stove more pleasant when she came in. It seemed a strangely Puritan attitude for a dog, I thought.

He had fallen asleep expecting the whine and scratch at the

door. But morning came and no Lady. He was too worried to go into town, but spent the morning calling and whistling for her. At noon he headed into the woods, looking for her tracks in the drifting cold and shouting her name. He started to think I had lured the dog away with grouse giblets. She had been gone nearly twenty-four hours when Banger, on fire with suspicion, came through my door.

At earliest light we cast out in ever-widening circles from Banger's sugarhouse. The wind was dying and new tracks held. There were no signs of Lady. I thought of Stone City and again saw Banger dropping the grouse viscera in the snow as he told me about the driving away of the Stones. Lady might have remembered where those forbidden morsels had fallen. A quick, guilty trip, a hurried gobbling, then back to scratch on the sugarhouse door and go to the comfort of the mat behind the stove. I guessed she might have run that number on Banger a dozen times.

"You already check Stone City?" I asked him.

"No, but she wouldn't go there unless we was huntin' birds."

"Might not hurt to take a look and be sure."

Banger was skeptical, morose, but we turned south, struggling and sinking in the drifts like men in quicksand.

The red bramble canes in the cellar holes rattled in the falling wind. Stone City was being washed away by waves of snow lapping up onto the random piles of boards, flooding the foundations, erasing the last traces of the Stones. The full tides of winter would drown the farm.

Banger kicked at the snow where he'd dropped the viscera. There was nothing there except ash from the fire staining the pale snow.

"Anything coulda picked 'em up—'coon, fox, fisher cat. Lady don't eat bird guts."

We cast around the field and along the brook. Banger called.

"See? Fox tracks, pretty fresh, too—this mornin's. That's what picked up them bird guts."

But then Banger was looking beyond the fresh fox tracks to a faint trail in the windswept snow, a shallow depression completely drifted over in the open, and, under the sheltering conifers, little more than a hint that something had dragged through earlier.

"What made that?" I asked. "Weasel, fisher cat? Something low-slung to make that trough." Banger looked at me with scorn and bitterness. He had seen that kind of trail before.

It led to the blackberry brambles that encased the lower Stone hayfields in bristling armor. Banger walked into the stout, thorned canes as though into a field of grass, muttering and talking to himself. I plowed along behind him, not understanding what he already knew with certainty.

He went down on his knees about fifteen feet into the canes and brushed the snow off the humped form of Lady. There were fox tracks circling the frozen body. Banger lifted the dead dog, but felt the resistance and laid her down again gently. He worked along the chain from the trap that held her right front leg to the snarl of links wrapped tight around the brambles. He opened the jaws of the trap and pulled out the stiff forepaw, then hurled the trap as far as he could into the brambles. It dangled from a thick clump of thorny canes, the chain bouncing in short, jaunty arcs.

"Banger!" I shouted. "Don't you want the trap to find out whose it is?"

His eyes glared from his purple face. He held Lady in his arms, heavy and frozen into a crooked caricature of dog shape. He hadn't said anything but now he screamed, "I know who done it! Old man Stone. He already done everything to me he could. He run me off here when I was a kid, shot me with a twelve-gauge, burned me out, yes he's the one burned up my Edie and the boy after I run them all out of Stone City, and now he's took my dog because I got his goddamn old knife! Here, you Stone, take it. Take it back. I don't want it."

He held the dog awkwardly with one arm while he dragged at his pocket, pulled out the old yellow knife and threw it down. He kicked at it, then started away to the sugarhouse.

The trap was a number two Blake and Lamb, nearly new. Under the smoked surface the aluminum name tag was still shiny. The stamped letters read "Raymond Pineaud, Jr." Raymie had again neglected his line. Even to the bastard descendants the Stones were predators. They could not help it any more than Banger, fluttering in suspicious apprehension, could help being their victim.

The hardware store was closed, then sold. I heard that Banger moved to Florida, to Arizona, to California, all earthly paradises to Chopping County. Raymie left on the bus for New York, his trapline rusting at its sets.

In the spring I sold my house to a retired couple from New Jersey. They were innocently enthusiastic about the country. While we were in the town clerk's office recording the sale, I asked, out of curiosity, who owned Stone City. The clerk searched it out.

"William F. Banger. He bought it years ago for the back taxes. He still owns it."

She was wrong. The Stones owned it and they always would.

The bastard fox loped smoothly down the hillside to the abandoned farm, carrying something delicately in his jaws. The den was a new one, an enlarged woodchuck hole that ran under a cellar foundation, the back entrance half-covered by a faded blue door.

The fox gently released his prize among his cubs. Despite its broken wing the year-old cock grouse tried to fly, but the smashed muscle and bone dragged and the bird rolled to the ground like a feathered pinwheel. The wooly cubs, still in milk teeth, cowered from the flapping terror. The bird ran, nearly gaining the brambles before the old fox caught it again, broke one leg and returned it to the cubs.

At last a small, ash-dark vixen, bolder than the others, darted for the bird and leaped away with a few blood-dabbled feathers.

Bedrock

MAUREEN split wood in the bare yard, surrounded by a circle of broken bark. A blue sheet of cloud marbled with heat lightning lay against the horizon.

From the spare room window Perley watched his young wife's braid of hair bounce with each stroke of the axe, her supple arms rise, the blade gleam like a sardonic smile in the air. She set a forked chunk on the block and scraped the earth with her foot. The axe rose and fell, the riven wood burst into two pieces with a ringing beat as though she had struck the stone shield beneath the earth.

Through the flawed window glass the field behind her seemed a piece of yellowed paper, poplar seedlings slashed across it like vertical pen strokes. This was the second season he'd missed the mowing. Perley looked at the field a hundred times a day. It was his habit to imagine how it might have been in other times; the primeval trees, the slope rough with smoking stumps, and wolves skulking through the dimmed landscape toward the emptier north. Now the tawny grass, streaked with milkweed and purple vetch, came halfway up Netta's stone that showed at the top of the hill like the white rising moon.

Maureen glanced over her shoulder and Perley jerked back. Missed him again, he thought; he was still quick. He shuffled away in his creased leather slippers, down to the kitchen to start supper. His sunburned farmer's color had faded months ago, and his pale, silver-stubbled face was as empty as the cat's licked saucer.

❦ ❦ ❦

At supper Maureen and Perley sat at the table, an empty yellow chair separating them. The forks stood tines up in a Sur-B-Gud coffee can. He wanted to get the right one. Maureen didn't like him to use the new forks with the stamped pattern of beaded roses and rampant vine.

She helped herself to the porkchops while Perley rested his hands on the tablecloth, smoothing the wooden handle of his knife. His mouth watered as she cut thick curls of butter. She looked at him, eyes the color of bluestone, signaled him to go ahead. He sawed the pale meat from the bone, the rivets in the handle of the knife winking in the light from the unshaded bulb. Maureen swallowed mouthfuls of the dark Brute potatoes. He wouldn't eat a blue potato. She could not make him do that.

After supper they watched static-streaked television until it was time to go up to the bedroom. He lay on his side of the bed in an old man's flickering sleep, watching the dry cracking of lightning without rain and the nervous green bursts of firefly incandescence across the fields. Maureen's breath was as slight as the new-risen wind in grass. Down along the river luminous cones of light spilled out of the summer houses. He watched the tangled skeins of lightning flush the hillside with a dead glare. Only when the blunt crumps of thunder moved on did the rain fall.

The farm was a thin mantle of soil that lay over granite bedrock scarred by glaciers and meteorites. The wineglass elms, the beech, the pad of stubbled grass, the interknotted roots, could all wash away again. Another deluge, he thought, would strip the rock bare, uncover the hard pit of the earth's core.

Atoms of this granite whirled in his body. Its stony, obdurate qualities passed up through the soil and into plant roots. Whenever he took potatoes from the heat-cracked bowl, his bones were hardened, his blood fortified. But Maureen, he knew, was shot through with some wild astral substance so hard and dense that granite powdered into dust beneath her blows.

•   •   •

When Netta died Perley split stone from the ledge behind the rock garden, striking the chisel over and over, hooking out the floury stone dust from the narrow holes. He set the shims and wedges, pounded them in until the stone broke from its bed with a dry, mild sound. He chiseled her name.

He hauled the finished marker up to the top of the field with the tractor. But when his daughter Lily saw it, she said the letters were too rough. They should have ordered a good polished stone carved with a verse and a design of flowers. She had clipped a poem out of a newspaper a few years ago and saved it for some reason. Now she knew why, she said.

Living by himself loosened him from his life. Once or twice in the kitchen he thought he heard Netta's low, dry voice asking him if he wanted ham for supper or not. The cat clawed her shriveled houseplants out of the pots to get at the dirt, and the crumbs of soil, sprayed over the carpet, seemed terrible to him in some obscure way.

It was Samuel, Lily's husband, with large heavy-lidded eyes like those of the marble busts of Roman emperors, who put the seed in his garden.

"You could marry again, you know."

They were mending fence, and the taut wire hummed as Samuel pounded in the staples. The fresh wind slapped against the crushed fields.

"Quite a few marry again. Been over a year. You're not throwed down in the weeds yet, Perley. You're still of an age where things can happen."

The women thought so, too. They brought casseroles and pies, jars of pears with cloves drifting like drowned men through the cloudy syrup. Selma Ruth, stuck with bringing up her wayward daughter's children, came with bread.

"I'll be darned if I let the state bring up any grandkids of mine," she said, limping away from his porch, the fresh-baked loaves lying on his outstretched palms like two sweet pillows. He imagined himself sitting at a table with children who rolled their peas around the racetrack of the plate rim. He wondered if he should tell them to stop or hope they'd grow out of it. Lily and Samuel had no children.

It was a very sharp, clear day when he began to lose the farm. Blackened weed stalks lay stiff on the frosted earth, brittle fallen leaves rolled in the shifting wind.

He recognized Bobhot Mackie's truck coming up from the river road, an old red Chevy with juddering fenders and bald tires, the splayed sides held in with a come-along. He went down the steps to see what Bobhot wanted, to keep him from getting out of the truck and running his hot, glaring eyes over the farm, looking for things to pick up later. Maureen, Bobhot's young sister, got out.

"Come to clean up for you, do some home cookin'."

Bobhot put his clubby elbow in the window and laughed, a sniggering bark, and the girl switched her long braid. Perley tried to say that he got everything up good by himself, but Bobhot took off, tooting the horn in bold blats, leaving her there.

The girl came to him that night, her unbraided hair heavy and hot. She was knowing, but meek, and her limbs folded into yielding positions at his lightest touch. The guilty scents of willow pollen and the river in spring flooded the room, the looming shape of the past was suddenly uncovered like a hand pulled away from a face. He seemed to feel drying mud beneath his nails.

They were married a month later during a snow squall, wind resonating the bell with a confused humming. He wore a white suit.

Lily had said, "This is disgustin'. It's the bride who wears the white, not a old man marryin' a girl four years younger than his own daughter."

The suit was the dense, slippery white of lard, and hung in caressing folds about his knotted legs when he tried it on in the store. But in the cold church it clung like wet plastic.

He stood again on nearly the same floorboard as during his first wedding. Then he had worn a black suit. Then it had been late afternoon in August, the beer-colored light falling through the same dusty glass; the silence, except for a wasp against the window, as thick, as felted as mullein leaves. That heat, the yellow light, Netta's blunt hand, the scent of musty piety seemed more real than the chilly ceremony that now bound the girl, Maureen, to him.

Lily and Samuel did not come to the wedding. "What a family you are bringin' into this one," Lily cried. "You have done the worse you could do." Only Bobhot was there, red and drunk.

Maureen scorned a honeymoon. She repapered the farmhouse with patterns of flowery trellises for the bedrooms, red teapots in the kitchen. She twisted up her long braid and painted the kitchen chairs yellow, the old oak table a cold green, like grass in the rain. Curtains printed with scarlet hibiscus hung in the lean farmhouse windows. Yet there were piles of dirty dishes in the sink, the grimy towel hung askew on a nail.

Bobhot came for dinner, ate hotdogs, one after another, his scalding eyes roaming around the room, lighting on the wallpaper, the clock shaped like a scottie dog, the plastic fern on the windowsill over the iron sink. He ate his Jell-O and left, and for long minutes they could hear the red Chevy rattling away down the river road.

Perley grew Green Mountain potatoes, the waxy yellow flesh very much to his taste. He had tried other kinds, Mortgage Lifter, Russet, Rose King, but never Brute. Never a dark blue potato, an inky, poison-looking thing.

"I'll have Bobhot send us over some seed potato," said Maureen in April.

"Don't need to, I got plenty stored."

"But not Brute."

"Green Mountain. I always grow Green Mountain."

"I like Brute. They are the best tastin' potato. I wouldn't give dirt for a Mountain." There was a bold note in her voice that astonished him. He laughed in disbelief.

"On this farm we grow Green Mountain." He was innocent of what would happen next.

Fire cracked in her eyes. She hit him on the cheek with a full, swinging blow that knocked him against the wall. She smashed his nose while he was still trying to stand up and catch his breath with the outrage of it. She was all over him, pummeling, hair-pulling, digging her knees into his kidneys. She rolled him onto his back and slapped openhanded.

"Say 'Brute,' " she panted, punching him in the ribs with hard, bruising blows. He could not hit her back. He got her wrists and held them with all his strength until his arms trembled with the strain. He felt her shift and force her knee between his legs. She doesn't care what she does, he thought, and he said "Brute."

He stayed out in the barn until late that night, until the cold sent him into the house. He went up the back stairs to Lily's old room and lay under the chenille spread. Dim starlight sifted into the darkness. He heard the floorboards whine. She came into the bed, naked, her braid undone.

"Mr. Perley," she whispered. Her hot breath scalded his sore face. Her fingers slid up and down his body until he rolled onto her with a groan of self-hatred. Before he fell asleep he promised to plant Brute potatoes.

After the gardens were in he took the stepladder into the orchard to thin out the June apples and was up in the dark leaves and spurred branches when she knocked the ladder out from under him.

"You old bastard," she said, watching him fall. "Why didn't you let Bobhot borrow the brushcutter?" He lay on the ground among the hard green apples and thought it was useless to tell her how Bobhot came to help himself to the brushcutter the night before, his truck parked down the road, slipping silently into the shed. Perley had heard the gas can go over, and when he went out with the flashlight, Bobhot's eyes shone in the dark like red studs.

Perley began to watch out for her, as wary as a cat that is sometimes smoothed, sometimes kicked. He couldn't hit her; he deserved what was happening.

A feeling grew that something was misplaced, and he looked vaguely through drawers and cupboards. In the kitchen he found a stack of yellowed recipe cards written out in Netta's familiar hand. He thought of biscuits, tried to make some, leveling the cup of flour with the knife blade as he had seen Netta do a hundred times. The smell of baking had its comfort.

More and more Maureen was the one who split wood, hammered at the broken door hasp on the shed. In the yellow field dark bramble patches boiled up.

Bobhot came often, to help Maureen, he said, then sat in the yellow chair between them eating pot roast. Once he fell asleep at the table, his mouth hanging open to show dark shreds of meat in his teeth. Maureen woke him and sent him up to the spare room, and Perley saw that he found his way easily.

"Be dangerous for him to drive back—hit some car full a kids," she said. All night long he heard Bobhot's snorts and breathing behind the wall, felt the red eyes looking through the headboard and thought of the bristly, full cheek, like a side of ham, rubbing against the white pillowslip.

On a September morning Bobhot came early, his truck clanging with a jumble of iron sounds. The sky was smooth as a washed stone. Bobhot put down the tailgate and pulled out metal pipes.

"He's goin' to paint," said Maureen. "This house is all peelin' away."

Bobhot twisted and pounded the pipes into connectors until scaffolding rose against the back of the house. Perley looked up at him, high under the eaves, standing on a plank. There was a sucking sound as Bobhot pried the lid off a paint can.

Perley started up the hill, punishing his breathlessness by walking faster. The cat picked through the wet grass, following him. In a few hundred feet she gave up and cried after him in her narrow voice.

Behind Netta's grave a section of the old stone wall had

spilled onto the ground. Milkweed, bladder campion and goldenrod grew here. To the east lay the Presidential Range, a pale
jagged edge against a paler sky, like a strip of torn paper. Wilter,
the mail carrier, had told him there were still lynx in the mountains. Perley pictured them, their long, serious faces and mutton-
chop whiskers framed by drooping tamarack branches as they
stood on shadowy limbs, their feet bunched together and their
backs arched like bows. He looked down at his house, small and
low, the scaffolding like black wire, Bobhot like an ant. The new
paint was the coarse yellow of highway signs.

He worked on the wall, chinking the dark crevices. The rough
granite stones locked into one another, their strength in their
passive weight.

When he came down at noon he looked critically at Bobhot's
work, saw missed strokes, drips on the window glass. The wind
was up and carried hundreds of balloon spiders into the glaring
yellow.

Painting the house gave Bobhot a position. He came now for
breakfast, looked around, his eyes pulling at things. He dulled
the chain saw, ran the lawnmower over a rock, stacked wood so
the pile collapsed and left it that way. He was always in the yellow chair, taking any fork he liked.

At night Perley said to Maureen, "I don't want Bobhot to
come here so much." Maureen's arms and legs stiffened.

"He's helpin' us. He's the only one gets anything done around
here. Now shut up and be glad you got help. He's gettin' somethin' done on this place while you just moon around."

Perley got up before daylight the next morning. He picked half
a bushel of late string beans and two bushels of tomatoes and set
the baskets in the kitchen for Maureen to can. In the shed he
sharpened axes, grass clippers, the nicked lawnmower blade,
anything that would take an edge. He hitched the brush-hog to
the tractor and began to grind away at the hillside. The blade tore
at the young seedlings.

The sun beat a quick, ceaseless tempo. He had forgotten to

wear his billed cap and felt his face burning, his lips cracked and dry. He glanced down at the house often, thinking Maureen might bring his cap and a jar of cold water dashed with vinegar.

At noon she got into the truck. His eyes followed the plume of dust down the river road, watched it turn toward Bobhot's place. At once it was lonely in the field, a pointless kind of loneliness. He stopped the tractor and walked down to the house for a drink. His swathes lay even across the hillside, curved to fit the contour of the hill like the sweep of a comb over a skull.

The kitchen was as cool and dark as a cave. He drank cold water from the faucet, let the liquid run across his mouth and sunburned face. He sat in the yellow chair, his legs trembling. The beans and tomatoes were still where he had set them, each with a halo of flies.

He went upstairs, gripping the bannister, to the spare room. It had been his room when he was a boy, and later, Lily's room. The large square floor was painted the shining grey of Job's tears. The ceiling was a narrow rectangle clamped between slanting knee walls, the distortion forced by the roof pitch. On the bed the pink chenille spread was turned down, showing the pillow cover cross-stitched with Dutch girls. He lay down, emptied of every feeling but tiredness.

The pulsing sound of the tractor coming off the hill woke him. White sunlight slammed through the window in a solid hot ray. His headache beat in rhythm with the engine. Bobhot, finishing the job for him.

Halfway down the stairs he had a dizzy spell. Tub water was running in the bathroom. He could smell Maureen's bath oil. In a minute his head cleared, but there was a sugary taste under his denture.

From the porch he looked up at Bobhot's crooked rows, saw the half-peeled saplings jutting from the soil like random-thrown lances. He couldn't see Netta's stone.

The pickup strained on the steep rise and he threw it into four-wheel drive, going straight up. It was what he thought. Bobhot, trying to mow around the stone, had angled the brush-hog awk-wardly. The stone lay broken, the fresh fracture as white as teeth, her name facedown on the ground.

Perley went straight to Lily's place. He had not seen his daughter since he had married Maureen ten months earlier. Lily had kept her distance, letting him feel her disapproval over the two miles that separated the farms. He knocked at the door though he knew she had seen him pull in.

"Well, what in heaven's name is wrong with you." Lily stared at his red face, the face, she thought, of an old ginger tom with snowy whiskers.

"A little sunburn."

"I should say!"

He didn't know how to begin.

"Lily."

"Father," she said, mocking his constrained tone. At last she had to say, "I'n see things are not too good."

He got it out. "I think them two are tryin' to take over the farm. Want you to come up and stay a week or so, see what you think."

She narrowed her eyes, the cords in her neck tightened. "You know I can't leave Sam on his own."

Perley knew what she meant: made your bed, now lie in it.

He took the long way back on the old woods road and stopped in a place where he could look down on the south side of the farm. Here he was, he thought, hanging around in the woods, staring at the farm like a hired man who'd just been booted off the place.

"That's it," he said to the windshield, driving the truck straight down the hill, bumping and heaving over the rough ground. The muffler caught on a mound of earth thrown up around a wood-chuck hole and dragged along, catching in the grass, until it hit a rock and tore away. He shot into the yard with a noise like a grader, ready to have it out with both of them, ready to hit Bobhot with the prybar he snatched up from behind the passenger seat.

The house was empty. Gone off again, probably down to

Ashtony where Bobhot would drink beer and eat potato chips and Maureen would look over everything in the stores before she bought a dish or a plastic doormat. The color of the tomatoes had deepened to the somber red that precedes rot. He waited for half an hour, then went out to the shed and found the Sakrete.

He mixed a little of it up and carried it in an empty coffee can up to Netta's broken stone. He troweled it onto the break and set the fallen stone in place. The excess Sakrete oozed out, and he wiped it away. "Netta," he said in a low, embarrassed voice. He could hear the brainless rasp of cicadas, as irritating as burrs. What could he say to Netta? What had he ever said to Netta? He saw a fox scat on the grave and kicked it away. He pulled at the weeds.

When there was nothing more to do with Netta's stone he went down and sorted the good tomatoes from the rotten. He got out the canning kettle, scalded the jars, rummaged under the stairs for the lids.

At dusk he ate supper alone. He used the first fork his hand touched. Shining jars of pulpy tomatoes cooled on the sideboard. The kettle was washed and put away, the counters wiped clean, the floor swept. It was after dark when he heard Bobhot's truck drive in and a door slam.

Bobhot came in, his face as dark as a smoked ham, eyes like bird's eyes, orange and inhuman. He started to climb the stairs.

"Where the hell do you think you're goin'?" said Perley. "And where's Maureen?"

Bobhot's face swelled and he turned toward Perley as if his shirt had caught on a nail.

"Meow!" screamed Bobhot. "Meow! Old cat." Spit flew out of his squared mouth. He stumbled against the yellow chair, slapped at it. Perley gripped the prybar.

Bobhot swung both his arms up grandly as though he were a conductor starting an orchestra on a stormy piece. The force whirled him to the left and he grasped the refrigerator, pressing his face to the cold white enamel. His dull voice mumbled, "Leave me be." A thin streak of saliva crawled down the white refrigerator.

"Leave you be, all right," said Perley. "In the mornin' when you're sober enough to stand up you get back down to your own place and stay there."

Bobhot did not hear him. He sank lower and lower. His eyes were shut and his mouth open, like a crooked funnel.

Perley took the prybar and the flashlight and went out to the barn to sleep. He got the blanket from the truck on the way.

The hay in the loft was three years old, but the sweet dry perfume of grass flooded the room still. He went to the little window and shut off the flashlight. He could see the car headlights on the river road—quite a few these days—where only three or four years ago hardly anyone went by after sunset. The Mackie farm was down there somewhere in the darkness along the river.

On the southern skyline there was an orange tinge, light from the mercury lamps in Ashtony, and he pictured Maureen sitting in a bar letting an ugly troublemaker rub up against her. At last he broke apart some bales of hay and made a bed.

Smothered shouting woke him. His cheek was against a dusty floorboard. He could not find the flashlight. He felt his way to the window and looked down into the lighted kitchen. Maureen leaned over Bobhot, shaking him, yelling into his face. In a few minutes she went upstairs, turning on the lights, flushing the darkness from the stairwell, from the empty rooms.

"I'm not there," whispered Perley.

Back down in the kitchen, she got Bobhot up. They swayed together as they climbed the stairs. Perley watched them go into the bedroom, watched them fall into the bed. The bedroom light went out, the one in the empty kitchen burned on. The embrace of Bobhot and Maureen was that of an old familiar couple.

Probably from the time they were kids, he thought. The Mackie kids, beaten, dressed in rags, fed on scraps he wouldn't give to pigs, clinging together like little monkeys for warmth and affection. He remembered them, years ago, out in the field digging potatoes when they should have been in school, thin kids scraped raw by the wind off the river.

They must have seen him, too, in his warm woolen jacket,

driving the shiny truck along the road with his little daughter beside him, must have seen the plump bags of grain in the back of the truck, or the new freezer. They stared at the house every time they went past the farm. And Netta had brought them down boxes of clothes that no longer fit Lily. "Dirty little things," she had said.

A car went along the river road and dwindled into the muffling darkness. In the empty kitchen intermittent flashes of light showed in the rhythmic drops that fell from the leaking faucet.

How easily things happened. It was ten or more years, he thought, since this part of his life had been set in motion, the first warm day after a grinding winter. He had let the cows out and they capered in the damp pasture as though the rare sunlight stung their crusted hides. He strode over the farm, kicking at the banks of coarse snow, not knowing what chore to start next. Jags and geese followed one another, their iron, ringing cries stirring his feeling of an incomplete life. He was fifty-nine, his flesh was still firm. The wind filled his mouth, as thick and warm as milk.

He remembered how he had felt, cutting across his land into Trumbull's woods, stumbling down toward the river. His boot heels left deep indentations in the mat of wet leaves. He came out in Mackie's fields. The snow was gone here and he crossed the leached rows of rotted corn stubble. The cold smell of melted snow came off the river. Ice cakes tilted on the black waves.

A girl stood holding a length of muddy clothesline tied onto a grappling hook. She watched the water. Two or three wet planks lay on the shore nearby, and he could see the drag marks where she had pulled them out. A wooden box rode down the current. She threw the hook with supple grace, but the wet box broke apart under the impact. He breathed in the thick fragrance of soil and wet bark. He could feel the beat of his blood in his swollen fingers.

"Water's pretty high, isn't it?" he said. Willow pollen streaked the child's face. Her eyes were some dark river color. She wore men's boots, worn out and patched, a muddy jacket. Her hair hung down in a long, thick braid. He knew who she was, the dirty little thing, but he said, "Now, what's your name?"

She made a short rush up the muddy bank on all fours, clawing at the dangling willow roots, her worn out boots gouging greasy scimitar-shaped marks in the clay. But when he pulled her down she was as slack and yielding in his grip as worn rope.

In the hayloft Perley folded his arms and leaned on the windowsill, waiting for morning. The empty illumination of the kitchen seemed to float in the darkness. He saw the yellow chair, stiff, awry, saw the iron sink as deep as an abyss. In the east the sky already showed a dull streak like a stony outcrop where the soil was washing away.

A Run
of Bad Luck

CLOUDS of steam rose from the kettle of boiling potatoes and condensed on the windows. Mae slid the big frying pan onto the hot front lid and knocked in a spoonful of bacon fat. When the pan smoked she laid in thick pieces of pork side meat. "If they want somethin' better, let them go out and get it," she said to the dog. She nudged him with her foot. "Go on, Patrick." He slouched away from the stove and fell under the table like an armful of wood. The meat curled at the edges and threw off a fine mist of grease.

Outside a truck door slammed. "Right on the button," said Mae, turning the pork. She was tall and stooped with smooth, wood-colored skin that made Haylett say "Indian" to her. She sawed the loaf of bread into thick slices and stacked them on a plate, set out a pound of butter already hacked and scored by knife blades.

Haylett and the two boys filled the low-ceilinged room. They pulled off their muddy pacboots and set them on the newspaper behind the stove, hung up the wool jackets that held the shapes of their shoulders, the bend of their arms. Haylett lathered his hands and forearms in the sink. Mae dipped out a pan of hot water from the stove reservoir, ran in a little cold water, and poured it over his head while he rubbed his face with both hands and snorted.

"Ray's not eatin' here tonight, Ma," said Phil.

"Where's he eatin', then?"

"Home. Says he's goin' out huntin' alone tomorrow and wants to get ready. He's not goin' with Amando and us."

✽✽✽

"Thinks he's goin' to get one by himself," said Clover.

"I imagine he'll try," said Haylett and scraped the chair legs over the floor. Mae set out the platter of meat and potatoes, a bowl of succotash.

"Looks like everybody gets the day off but me," she said. The three men leaned over their plates, shoving the food into their mouths. Phil shook pepper over everything.

"Don't anybody notice they're eatin' pork for the third straight week?" she said. "Seems like you'd notice that."

"Wait'll tomorrow," said Phil, "there'll be four bucks hangin' out there."

"Shut up," said Clover, "you ruin the luck talkin' about it." His slow glance went to the shelf where his buck lures stood, Dr. T's Buck Urine, Hunter's Moon Doe-In-Heat, and Rawhide Gel.

"Shut up yourself," said Phil. Haylett scraped his chair back and forth for silence. Mae put a potato on his plate.

"What's takin' Amando so long? He didn't go over to the trailer, did he, tryin' to get back with Julia?"

"I imagine," said Haylett, "I imagine it's about the road. He's had to go see about the road. I told him we ought not skid logs when it was that wet, wait until it froze up again, but no, Amando and Ray was in a hurry to get done."

"When was this?"

"About two weeks ago, after all that rain. It was the last day on Warp's lot if we pulled the logs out then. If we left 'em, we'd of had to come back with all the equipment, break into the setup we got now over on the Cold Key Road. Amando says, 'Don't worry about it. If anybody squawks I'll take care of it. Let's get these logs out now.' "

"Yeah," said Mae, "I can just hear him sayin' it."

"So today here comes Benny, says, 'Selectmen want to talk to you boys about what you done to town highway number six.' I didn't say a word, just waved him over to Amando. Let him talk his way out of it, he's such a good talker."

"Is it rutted up bad?"

Phil laughed, jerking his head back, a single hard noise that came out of his throat like a bird cry. "Rutted up bad? It's a lake, a lake all filled up with brown water. Fish could live there. You could swim across." He thrust up his arm to show the depth, and fragments of food fell from his fork into his hair.

"Well, there's not much they can do about it, is there. Whyn't they just fix it up and leave him alone," said Mae. She made up a plate for Amando with an extra slice of meat, mashed his potato fine with her fork and shaped it into a cup to hold the gravy. She put the plate into the warming oven, made a cup of tea for Haylett.

The boys started in on opening day. Mae guessed they'd talked about it since morning, where they might go, whether to track or still hunt or drive, reviewing past seasons and deer sign they'd seen in the last few weeks.

"You make brown bread, Ma?" asked Clover.

"You know I didn't. I been a workin' girl since July, if you'd notice, and you're lucky I get back here in time to make dinner. There's a pie. Whyn't you take pie? Apple or cherry."

"Ma, I like to have the brown bread. You don't know how good it is when you're half froze and starved. And it don't flash white like a sandwich or pie."

"It takes three hours of slow steamin' to cook brown bread, and I'm about ready to hit the hay right now."

"I'll stay up and watch it," said Clover. "I don't want to get shot by some flatlander thinks a white sandwich is a buck's behind like that guy got killed over on Hawk Mountain. Brown bread brings me good luck."

"Knowin' what you're doin' brings the luck, mister man," said Haylett.

"That guy on Hawk Mountain," said Phil. "Like this." He leaned back, put one foot on the chair, whistled carelessly and bit an imaginary sandwich. He bit again, the imaginary sandwich flew away, the teeth thrust from the contorted mouth and his hand jerked up as though to stop a hot spray of blood jetting out of his throat.

They heard Amando's truck outside, heard the door to the

shed slam. Amando came into the kitchen on a wedge of raw air, stamping his feet. They watched him pull the knitted cap off his sand-colored hair, tight round curls like a drawing; like a drawing too, his heavy eyelids and amber irises so pale they seemed the color of bog water. The narrow, handsome face was marked with fine lines. Mae took his heavy jacket and hung it with the others behind the stove.

"Turnin' colder out?" said Haylett. A sense of unease seeped into the kitchen with the bitter air, a feeling that it was necessary to watch out for something. Phil put his head down and ate pie.

"Snow. Smells like snow. I kept lookin' for snow on the windshield all the way here. And the damn heater in the truck don't work." Amando jerked his chair out and sat at the table.

"Trackin' snow," said Clover. "I hope we get three or four inches of good trackin' snow."

Phil dragged his fork across his plate. "What'd the selectmen say, Amando, what'd little bowlegged Benny and the selectmen say?"

Mae set Amando's plate in front of him. He looked directly at her, something her other sons rarely did. Haylett, never. Amando ate without answering.

"Clover," said Mae, "you're so eager for brown bread, how about you get a start on the dishes while I mix it up?" Amando looked up.

"You ain't goin' to start makin' brown bread now, are you?"

"I wouldn't, only Clover wants it bad enough to set up while it steams. I'm goin' to bed just as soon as I get it on the stove." She began mixing the molasses and eggs in a heavy yellow bowl. Clover slid the plates through the greasy water and Phil sang made-up words nobody knew.

Something made Haylett look up. He was writing his daily lines on the weather in his pocket notebook, *sun a.m. wet sharp wind out of sw, cloudy by 4, shower, dark by 5*. His pencil stopped. "Is that sleet or snow," he said, hearing the scattered ticks on the window glass. Phil pressed his hot face against the window. "Sleet," he said, watching the spicules of ice slide down the pane. Haylett's pencil wrote.

Haylett was down the next morning at three-thirty to get the stoves going. He liked turning the dark chill away, enjoyed the little solitude, the resinous odor of kindling catching fire. The shovel squeaked as he drew out the ashes.

Mae yawned into the kitchen in her old pink chenille wrapper, the back shiny where she'd sat it flat, held her hands over the crackling stove in the ritual gesture to catch the first comforting warmth. There was Haylett with his billets of wood and chunking damper balancing chimney draft against the quick need for heat.

The brown bread was still faintly warm. She sliced it and wrapped the pieces in foil, cut the remains of a pork roast, leaving the white rim of fat on the meat, making the deer-hunt lunches the way she'd made them for thirty years, packing in the sweet, fatty foods they liked. Clover would have nothing pale nor white, nothing that cracked when bitten, nothing too juicy. "Too bad they don't make black cheese," she murmured.

Haylett put the coffee on, an electric plug-in pot Amando and Julia had given them at Christmas a year ago. The novelty was still on it; they thought it a luxury to drink the fresh hot coffee before the kettle on the wood-fired kitchen range boiled. She slid the big frying pan onto the hot spot and knocked in a spoon of bacon grease. She had saved the coffeepot wrapping paper, dark green with silver bells on it. Something Julia picked out.

Clover galloped through the kitchen and out into the dark in his bare feet, hand clamped over his groin, eyes blind with sleep. He came back salted with fine, hard crystals. "Still comin' down. If it stops pretty soon we'll be okay. Put the radio on, Pa, let's see if we can get the forecast." He poured a cup of coffee and took it upstairs with him. They heard him kick Phil's door, say, "Get up or get left." The radio crackled and blurred, snatches of music whirled past as Haylett twisted the dial.

"Here, let me do that. You always rip through those stations like the knob was hot." Mae found the school report station she'd tuned in for years when the boys were in school to tell when they could stay home instead of hiking a mile down the road in bad weather. The familiar racy voice surged at them. ". . . off tonight. Total accumulation six to eight inches, up to twelve inches in the mountains. And on Mount Washington the temperature is thirty-seven below with winds gusting to seventy. . . ."

"Dammit, I hate to go huntin' when it's snowin'. Tracks get covered up, can't see nothin', deer all bed down in the cedars, you can step on one before it'd get up and move, your clothes get wet, you can't see where the boys are or what trigger-happy hunter from New Jersey is out there ready to shoot blind at the first sound he hears."

"Stay home then. Get right back in bed." She filled the four worn thermos bottles with coffee. "That's it. Got to make another pot."

"How are you gettin' home tonight?" he asked.

"Tess is pickin' me up and Tess is droppin' me off. You don't have to pick me up today."

The bulb over the sink gave off a tepid light. The kitchen was filled with the stunned silence that comes with the first snow. Mae suddenly called up the stairs, "You, Phil, you put on your long johns." She waited until she heard bureau drawers slamming and Phil's muttered voice, and went back to the stove. The eggs cracked into the pan, she shook pepper onto their gleaming breasts.

Haylett ate standing up beside the stove and went out to start the truck. He liked a warm truck, let it run three-quarters of an hour sometimes. Mae appreciated that about him, the way he never let her or anyone get into a cold truck and sit shivering while the engine bleated and failed. "Worth somethin', isn't it," she said to old Patrick who was lying in front of the stove again. "Don't come cryin' to me if you get hot grease on your back."

Amando came down, his curly hair flaring, his face still drawn and sad with sleep. The waffle weave of his underwear showed at the neck of his heavy plaid shirt. He drank his coffee without talking, head bent, shoulders drawn forward.

"What's wrong with you this mornin'?" she said. He shook his head and put up his hand.

"You look down in the dumps. You thinkin' about gettin' back with Julia?"

"No, Ma. I told you over and over, she's gettin' a divorce." His voice was light and hard.

"She hasn't got it yet," said Mae. "Amando, she hasn't got it yet. You can turn it around. I always liked Julia."

Through the window they could see the taillights of the truck coloring the gushing exhaust red, see Haylett's legs light up like cherry neon when he came around the back of the truck to the shed door. He came into the kitchen, grown larger against the cold, his voice heavy and braced. There was snow in his hair. "Wind is pickin' up," he said. "Won't see shit today, but I suppose we got to try it."

Phil and Clover folded slices of bread around their eggs. A gust of wind shook the house, drove the snow against the clapboards like pins. Something outside, the garbage can cover, hurled along, stuttering metal. A sound like a fall of water into a chasm came as snow slid off the roof. Haylett turned to Amando.

"Don't forget to leave Mero's check for your mother so she can make the skidder payment and work out the wages. Ray will want to be paid tonight."

Phil pantomimed Ray's delight with his wages by tipping an imaginary bottle into his mouth and making a hollow gurgle in his throat.

"Goddammit, why don't you eat and quit horsin' around!" shouted Amando. He looked over at Mae but she knew by the cant of his voice he was talking to his father. "Mero's check is up on the bureau. Might as well know that pursey little gang of selectmen give me a bill for road damages yesterday." Haylett, pouring his last cup of coffee, tightened up.

🐟🐟🐟

"How much?"

"You don't want to know."

"How much?"

"Twelve hundred." Amando's mouth turned down like a metal hook. His furious eyes fastened at a point on the wall.

"Jesus Christ, that's our whole profit for the job!" Haylett threw the coffee in the sink. The dog, Patrick, slunk guiltily under the table at the sound of shouting.

"I know that!" Amando said. "They're crazy. Three truckloads of gravel is all they need to dump up there, smooth it out with the grader. Fifty-five a load for the gravel if I was to get it at Cannon's, twelve if the town buys it. The whole thing shouldn't cost more than two hundred. I told 'em I'd pay for puttin' the road back the way it was, but no way was I goin' to pay twelve hundred."

"What'd they say, what'd Sonny say?"

"You got it right. The rest of 'em said nothin'. Sonny said they'd take it to court."

No one spoke. The falling snow, the wind, gradually seized their attention again. Clover and Phil bent low, putting on their boots. Mae scraped the plates furiously.

"Might as well get goin'," said Haylett. "You ridin' with us?" Amando worked the muscles in his jaw.

"No. I'll take my truck and follow you. It's good to have two trucks up there in bad weather."

Phil and Clover went up to get the rifles from the gun cabinet, the hauling straps and knives.

"He's gonna jump on me once too often," said Phil on the stairs.

"It's Sonny he's mad at, not you."

"Yeah? He's mad at everybody." He said it loudly so they'd hear him in the kitchen.

"You shouldn't of snapped at Phil that way," said Mae. "He didn't mean nothin' by it. He's just at that stage to make fun of everything."

Amando stamped into his boots. "He gets on my nerves. Dad

gets on my nerves. It's drivin' me up the wall the way things are goin', this rotten luck. All this year I had bad luck with everything I touch. My wife quits me. I got this goddamn toothache keeps comin' back. The heater in the truck don't work good, and now this thing with the road on top of the rest of it. By god, I can use a day of huntin', snow or not. Way things are goin', lucky if I get a spikehorn."

Men came from other states to see Amando's collection of antlers. He had shot a buck every year since he was twelve. No rack had less than eight points. They were all nailed onto the side of the garage he and Ray had built over at the trailer where Julia now lived alone. When Clover was little he had asked Amando to give him the collection when he died.

"When I die?" said Amando, staring at the boy as if he couldn't believe what he was hearing. "I am *never* goin' to die," he said, "but in case I do, my antlers is goin' to be buried with me. I just can't decide if I should have them piled up underneath or set on top. You'll have to get your own."

Clover had imagined that mound of shining bone, tines and points locked into a huge ivory ball, balanced on his brother's dead body. Amando would lie as flat and white as a piece of paper, the weight of the antlers pressing him down into the yielding soil until hunter and trophies all descended to the core of the earth and sifting red pine needles covered the place where they had been.

Haylett, Clover and Phil sat packed into the hot truck, thighs and shoulders touching. The windshield wipers swept to and fro, one of the best sounds in the world, thought Clover. Phil, stiff as a fence post, stared out the side window, his eyes scratching the darkness.

"I wish he'd move back with Julia, get out of the house."

Clover felt calm and remote in the heat, his leg drawing strength from his father, his arm locked against his brother's. The morning light was still a long time away. They would have to walk in the darkness to get in place.

"It's his bad luck that makes him that way."

"*He* thinks it's bad luck," said Haylett, turning onto Dogleg Road, the truck slewing in the new snow.

"What is it then?" said Phil. "Good luck?"

"Don't get smart," said Haylett. "It's his life. It's the way his life is turnin' out, and he don't know it yet."

The road went on up toward the height of land where the trail, overgrown, visible only to the experienced eye, branched off and ran along the ridge. Below lay the great cedar swamp, miles of brush and hummocks, brackish water and blowdowns. A drive through this low ground sent the deer crashing up onto the ridge. Eight of Amando's racks and Clover's first buck had come from those heights.

"Are we goin' past the trailer, Dad?"

"Have to, unless you want to fly. You know that."

The truck went steadily on, the beams of light before them filled with hurling snow. The plow had not been through, and there were no other tracks on the road, covered with the voluptuous, curving snow. Haylett was relieved. Each year he dreaded to find someone else was working the swamp before they got there.

The truck came abreast of the trailer and they all looked toward the antlers on the garage, looked to see if the trailer had somehow changed in the weeks since Julia had ordered Amando away for a reason no one knew.

"She isn't goin' to get the antlers, is she, Dad?" said Clover.

"Oh Jesus Christ," said Haylett, slowing down.

They saw Julia's Datsun in the driveway, and right behind it, Ray's scabby blue pickup. There were tall hats of snow on both vehicles. Then they were past and the trailer dropped out of sight behind them. Haylett stopped the truck beyond the next rise. They sat there, engine pulsing, windshield wipers batting, batting.

"Maybe he just stopped by for a cup of coffee," said Phil.

"Yeah, drinkin' it there in the dark all night long. Look at the snow on his truck," said Clover.

Haylett backed the truck, then began to inch forward in a tight turn that made the steering linkage give short emotionless shrieks.

"What are you gonna do?" said Phil.

"Get turned around and down the road before Amando comes along and sees that pickup in his yard. We're goin' to tell him there's flatlanders up here drivin' the swamp. We'll go up to Athens instead and hunt those old orchards. We always said we'd go up there sometime." They heard the tremor in his voice. The truck's rear wheels dropped down into the deep ditch that lay under the deceptive snow. Haylett stepped on the accelerator and the tires spun as though they were in oil.

"Get out and push, and get some back into it," he cried. Clover and Phil ran behind the truck and braced themselves against the tailgate. The tires spun in a nasal whine. They heaved at the truck, and mud mixed with snow shot onto their legs. Haylett rocked it back and again the tires spun. He jumped out and began pulling at deadwood along the roadside, stuffing bark and branches under the wheels. He found a rotten fence post and kicked it under, a length of rusty barbwire trailing.

"This time it's goin' out," he said. "Never mind pushin', just get in the back and keep your weight over the wheels."

"Go!" shouted Phil. The wood pieces shot out behind the truck, the tires gouged trenches in the side of the ditch, and they were back on the road.

Clover and Phil crouched in back, the bitter snow stinging their faces. We're in it now, thought Clover, as they whipped past the trailer, sliding in their own tracks, toward the yellow glow of Amando's headlights coming up the hill.

The two trucks drew abreast of each other and lay side by side, their engines pulsing softly in neutral like two boats in a white channel. From the drivers' windows came clouds of breath that met and mingled in the hollow air between them.

"What's wrong?" In the reflected light Amando's eyes were colorless and transparent.

"Got a crowd of flatlanders up there workin' the swamp.

Thought we'd better turn around and go up to Athens today, try those orchards we always said we would."

Amando looked at Phil and Clover in the back of the truck. "What're they doing back there, road huntin' or gettin' some fresh air?"

"We got stuck turnin' around. Come on up front, boys," he yelled, "you might as well be warm."

"Well then," said Amando. He was wary now, feeling something. The trucks throbbed. "I'll just go up and turn around in my old driveway."

"Turn around here, no need to go wake up Julia. Let's get down the road."

Amando stared at his father. It's no good, thought Clover, no good at all. The hair on the back of his neck felt rough, as if there were a loose snake on the cab floor. He could feel a rapid tremble in Haylett's leg. Amando touched his accelerator and the throaty snort of the truck was like a blunt, filthy word. He shifted into first, and his receding taillights drew a red band across Haylett's face. Everything that happens, thought Clover, happens in trucks, remembering a neighbor's pickup jouncing crazily across a stubbled hayfield toward them years before, the woman crying to them as she drove, and on the seat beside her, already dead, the bee-stung child.

"He'll shoot 'em both," cried Phil.

"Shut up." Haylett turned the engine off. They sat with the windows open, straining to hear. The windshield wipers lay limp against the glass. They heard the hiss of the snow in the brush beside the road, the faint muffled sound of Amando's truck. They heard their own ragged breathing. The cooling metal of the truck's hood ticked.

What's happening now, thought Clover, was already happening this morning and I couldn't see it. Haylett's trembling leg was like old Patrick's guilty tremor when someone shouted at him. Clover saw that Haylett, in begetting Amando, had created this snow-filled morning in a silent truck. A sense of the mysterious force of generation rushed in on him.

The trees behind them filled with light, and then the rear window flared yellow.

"He's comin' back," said Phil. Amando's truck came slowly along until it drew up beside them again. Clover could hear a piston knock. Amando got out and came over to Haylett's window. He leaned in, and the raw smell of fresh snow came off him like smoke.

"You thought I didn't know," said Amando.

Haylett trembled like a taut wire fence struck with a stick. He nodded, the trembling head dipping, nodding.

"Oh, I knew," said Amando, and pulled away from the window, leaving the black morning and the random, crisscrossing snow in his place.

Heart Songs

SNIPE drove along through a ravine of mournful hemlocks, gravel snapping against the underside of the Peugeot. He had been driving for an hour, past trailers and shacks on the back roads, the yards littered with country junk—rusty oil drums, collapsed stacks of rotten boards, plastic toys smeared with mud, worn tires cut into petal shapes and filled with weeds. He slowed down to look at these proofs of poor lives the same way other drivers gaped at accidents on the highway, the same way he had once, years before, looked out a train window into a lighted room where someone sprawled naked on a mattress, a hand reaching for a cheap bottle.

He sucked at his thin lower lip, watching for the turn to the left. He was bony, with a high-colored face and bloodshot, dim, gooseberry eyes set in shallow sockets. His pale reddish hair receded in front, grew long behind his ears, as though his scalp had slipped back a little each year. Women were sometimes pulled to him despite the stooped shoulders and the way his nervous, bitten fingers picked at his face or tapped against each other's tips in fretful rhythms. A sense of dangerous heat came from him, the heat of some interior decay smoldering like a lightning-struck tree heart, a smothered misery that might someday flare and burn.

It was two years since he had left his wife for Catherine, the city for the country, the clothing shop that his wife now successfully ran alone for sleazy jobs in unfamiliar places. He'd quit the last three weeks ago, sick of dipping old furniture into a tank of stinking paint remover. Now he had the fine idea to play his guitar in rural night spots, cinder-block buildings on the outskirts of town filled with Saturday night beer drunks and bad music. He wanted to hook his heel on the chrome rung of a barstool, hear the rough talk, and leave with the stragglers in the morning's small hours. He recognized in himself a secret wish to step off into some abyss of bad taste and moral sloth, and Chopping County seemed as good a place as any to find it.

He came out of the hemlocks into brushy, tangled land and missed the narrow track hidden in weeds at the left. He had to back up to make the turn at the rusted mailbox leaning out of the cheatgrass like a lonesome dog yearning for a pat on the head. The guitar sounded in its case as Catherine's car strained up the grade, alder and willow whipping the cream-colored finish. The potholes deepened into washouts and shifting heaps of round, tan stones. He passed an old pickup truck abandoned in a ditch, its windshield starred with bullet holes, thick burdocks thrusting up through the floor. Snipe felt a dirty excitement, as though he were looking through the train window again. When the Peugeot stalled on the steep grade he left it standing in the track, though it meant he would have to back down the hill in the dark.

He felt the gravel through the thin soles of his worn snakeskin boots; the guitar bumped against his leg, sounded a muffled chord. A quarter of a mile on, he stopped and again took out the creased letter.

Dear Sir, I seen your ad you wanted to play with a Group. I got a Group mostly my family we play contry music. We play Wed nites 7 pm if you want to come by.
—Eno Twilight

A map, drawn with thick pencil lines, showed only one turn off the gravel road. He folded it along the original creases and put it back in his shirt pocket so it lay flat and smooth. He'd come this far, he might as well go all the way.

The grade leveled off and cornfields opened up on each side

of the track. A mountaintop farm. Godawful place to live, thought Snipe, panting and grinning. He could smell cow manure and hot green growth. Pale dust sprayed up at every step. He felt it in his teeth, and when his fingers picked at his face, fine motes whirled in the thick orange light of the setting sun. A hard, glinting line of metal roof showed beyond the cornfield, and far away a wood thrush hurled cold glissandos into the stillness.

The house was old and broken, the splintery grey clapboards hanging loosely on the post-and-beam frame, the wavery glass in the windows mended with tape and cardboard. A hand-painted sign over the door said GOD FORGIVES. He could see a child's face in the window, see fleering mouth and squinting eyes before it turned away. *Arook, arook,* came a ferocious baying and barking from the dogs chained to narrow lean-tos beside the house. They stood straining at the edges of their dirt circles and clamored at his strangeness. Snipe stood on the broken millstone that served as a doorstep. Threads of corn silk lay on the granite. He was let into the stifling kitchen by the child whose uncontrolled face he had seen.

The stamped tin ceiling was stained dark with smoke, a big table pushed against the wall to make more room. Above it hung a fly-specked calendar showing a moose fighting off wolves under a full moon. The Twilights sat silently on kitchen chairs arranged in a horseshoe row with old Eno at the center. Their instruments rested on their knees, their eyes gleamed with the last oily shafts of August sunlight. No one spoke. The old man pointed with his fiddle bow to an empty chair with chromium legs and a ripped plastic seat off to the side. Snipe sat in it and took his guitar out of its case.

Eno Twilight's thick yellow-white hair was matted and clumped like grass in a November field, his face set in deep, mean lines. His fiddle was black with age and powdered like a sugar cake with rosin dust. He pointed his bow suddenly at the overalled farmer who sat wheezing an accordion in and out, its suspirations like the labored breathing of someone dying. "Give me a A, Ruby." The major chord welled out of the accordion and the old man twisted his fine-tuning screws delicately. Without a word or signal that Snipe could see, they began to play. It was new to Snipe, but a simple enough progression to follow. He slid in a little blues run that got him a cold look from old Eno.

"Just a piece of wedding cake beneath my pillow . . ." sang the girl in a hard, sad voice. The sun was gone and the room filled with dusk. The girl was fat, richly, rolling fat, and dressed in black. Her face was beautiful, with broad, high cheekbones and glittering black eyes. Genghis Khan would have loved her, thought Snipe, loving her himself for the bleakness of her voice. Ruby would be her brother, with the same broad face and heavy body. His accordion made a nasal, droning undernote like bag-pipes, broken every few bars by circus music phrases, flaring, brassy elephant sounds. The effect was curious but not disagree-able. It gave the music a sardonic, rollicking air, like Long John Silver dancing a hornpipe, his wooden leg dotting blood on the captured deck.

Snipe introduced himself after the song ended and gave them a broad, glad-hand smile like a proof of good intent. They didn't care who he was, barely looked at him, and he darkened with em-barrassment. Again, without warning, they began to play. "Rules was made to be broken," sang fat Nell, and old Eno laid his cruel face onto the fiddle and set a line of cloying harmony against her pure voice.

After a few songs Snipe was excited. They were good. Old Eno played with extraordinary virtuosity, complicated rhythms and difficult bowings, his left hand moving fluidly up and down the fingerboard instead of locking into first position as many back-country players did. Shirletta, his wife, thin as a wire, grey hair in grey plastic curlers, twitched her little mouth and rang her man-dolin like a dinner bell.

The songs rolled out, one after another, with only a few sec-onds between each one. Snipe didn't know any of them. "What's that called?" he would ask at the end of a tune, and the Twilights would stare at him. Someone would mumble, "The Trout's

Farewell," or "Wet Hay," or "There's a Little Gravestone in the Orchard," or "Barn Fire," the last a ramping, roaring jig with harmonic yodeling by all the Twilights at such speed that Snipe could only hang on and clang the same chord for six full minutes. "Why haven't I heard that one before?" he cried. "Who does it?" No one answered him.

At nine the old man looked over and said, "Well, it's time," and the Twilights obediently laid their instruments aside. Snipe's fingers throbbed from hours of playing without a break. The hot kitchen had made him thirsty, but Eno said, "Good night. Next Wednesday same time if you want to come. You ain't too bad, but we don't go in for that fancy stuff." Snipe knew he meant the blues run.

"Listen, where do you play?" asked Snipe.

"Right here," said the old fiddler, giving him a look as hard as knots in applewood.

"No, I mean, where do you play dances, play out, whatever. *Gigs,* you know?"

"We don't play out."

"You don't play anywhere but here? Nowhere else?"

"Nowhere else. We make a joyful noise unto the Lord." He turned away toward an inner doorway where fat Nell stood in the dim light. Snipe thought he had heard mockery in the old man's voice.

He would have skipped down the dark track lit by the bobbing circle of his flashlight, but he was afraid of breaking his legs. He felt charged with energy. These were real backwoods rednecks and he was playing with them. They were as down and dirty as you could get, he thought. Before he backed down the hill in the darkness, he held the flashlight in his teeth and scribbled all the songs he could remember on the back of Eno's letter: "The Road Accident," "Trumpled in a Fight," "Silver Hooves." Good, authentic rural songs. The real stuff. Where had the Twilights heard them? Seventy-year-old records as thick as pies? Old Eno's childhood radio memories? Local dances? The car cracked over the stones in the night. Snipe sang, "Just a piece of wedding cake beneath my pillow," in a slow, honking voice. His headlights shone in the green eyes of cats in the ditches as he drove back to his rented house.

The house was on a lake, and as he coasted down the drive, lined with its famous sixty-year-old blue Atlas cedars, he could see light from the living room window falling on the water like spilled oil. The car ticked hotly as he stood in the darkness. Under the slap of the waves against the dock he caught the monotonous pitch of mechanical television voices, and went inside.

Catherine sat in the tan recliner. Her eyes were closed and the desolate fluttering blue light mottled her tired face and the white shirt printed with a dancing dog and the words Poochie's Grill. Snipe turned off the lurching images and she opened her pale eyes. She was thin, a mayonnaise blonde with very light blue eyes like transparent marbles. Surly, ugly, she had a flat rump and beautiful strong legs with swelling calves. She was also getting tired of being broke, getting close to sniffing out Snipe's longing for a gutter.

"You got the job, I hope," she said.

"Ahhh," said Snipe, grinning like a set of teeth on a dish, "there really wasn't any job after all. We just played. But some very fine country stuff." He tried to pump some of the old, boy-genius enthusiasm into his voice, to imitate the confident manner he'd used with Catherine two years before when they sat up until three in the morning drinking expensive wine she had bought and making plans for living by selling bundles of white birch logs tied with red ribbon to fireplace owners in New York City, or growing ginseng roots they would sell through a friend whose brother knew a pharmacist in Singapore. "Cath, this is an undiscovered group and there's money there, big bucks—records, promotions, tours. The works. This could be the one, baby, it's the one that could get us on the way." He couldn't keep the secret revulsion at the thought of success out of his voice. At once she was furious and shouting.

❦ ❦ ❦

"My god, no job! Gas and money wasted. I work my butt off down in that kitchen"—she plucked at her Poochie's Grill shirt with disgust—"while you bum around playing free music. The rent on this place with its dismal rotten trees is coming up next week and I haven't got it, and I'm not borrowing from my parents again. It's your turn, buddy. Rob a bank if you have to, but you pay the rent!"

Snipe knew she would get the money from her parents. "What's so goddamn tough about making a few hamburgers to keep the ship floating?" he said. "I've got to build up my musical contacts here before I can expect to make any money. It takes time, especially in the country. It's more important I'm doing something I really like, you know that." He couldn't say to her that what he liked was the failing kitchen chair, the wrecked pickup in the weeds.

"Something *you* really like," sneered Catherine.

Snipe was tired of the effort to cajole her. "Listen, bitch, you forget very conveniently about the months I worked in that butcher shop where nobody had more than two fingers so you could learn Peruvian weaving. Whatever happened to the Peruvian weaving scam, anyway? Remember, you were going to make a lot of money by weaving serapes or bozos or whatever for Bloomingdale's?"

Catherine's failure to make any money at weaving was a dangerous subject. She flared up again. "You know they wanted indigenous Peruvian. I couldn't help it if I didn't live in a filthy hut on top of the Andes, could I? They didn't want Vermont Peruvian." She glared at Snipe with a horrible expression that reminded him of an early psychology book he had once seen with photographs illustrating the emotions: Catherine was HATE.

Snipe wrenched a beer from the row in the refrigerator after shaking the empty scotch bottle and went out onto the dock. There were more Atlas cedars along the shore, their long arms hanging forlornly over the water. He looked across the lake at the winking lights along the road and drank his beer, feeling a pleasant pity rising in him. He wondered how much longer Catherine would last. She was spoiled by her rotten-rich mother and father, their soft lips folded, their soft hands slipping an envelope into her purse, not looking at him, writing letters that Catherine hid under the breadbox, long convoluted letters offering her trips to South America to study native weaving techniques, offering a year's rental of a little shop in Old Greenbrier where she could sell the heavy mud-colored cloaks and leggings she made, offering her vacations with them in the Caribbean, but never mentioning Snipe's name or existence. She'd leave him sometime. He thought about the Twilights on their mountain farm at the end of a bad road, turning the earth, sowing seed, and in the evening singing simple songs from their hearts in the shabby kitchen, poor enough so no one cared what they did. The idea came to him that they must have made up all the rueful, hard-time songs themselves, songs that no one heard.

There really could be an album, he thought, and maybe he could really guide them through the sharky waters of country-music promotion. They would wear black costumes, completely black except for a few sequins on the sleeves, black to set off the simplicity of their faces. The album cover would show a photograph of them standing in front of their ratty house, sepia-toned and slightly out of focus, rural and plain, the way he had told Catherine their own lives would be when they came to the country. Simple times in an old farmhouse, Shaker chairs by the fire, dew-wet herbs from a little garden, and an isolation and privacy so profound he could get drunk and fall down in the road and no one would see.

But all the old farmhouses had been made over into doctors' vacation homes with eagles over the door and split-rail fences. There wasn't anything to rent until Catherine's mother found "Cedar Cliffs," a modernistic glass horror stinking of money and crowded by forty mammoth blue Atlas cedars set out at the turn of the century. The owners were friends of Catherine's parents, and the deal went through before Snipe even saw the place and its melancholy arboretum. They were allowed a reduced rent of

$300 a month because it was understood that Snipe would tend the great shaggy branches and clean up the litter of twigs and cones that fell from them in a constant rain.

Snipe went to the Twilights' every Wednesday. He said nothing to them about an album. Each time was like the first time, the same chair, the same headlong rushes into the next unknown tunes, the same closed silence with no talk of the music or the way it was played, just on and on in the gathering dusk. Snipe was carried along by the sound, he played in tune and on time, yet he rode on top of the music like a boat on a wave because old Eno wouldn't make room for him, would not let them open the set pattern of their songs even a crack to let him play a riff or break or move out a little from the body of sound. Snipe, the outsider, was cast into a background corner, a foreign tourist who did not know the language, who would not stay, who was only passing through.

He kept on trying to belong to them by cawing enthusiastically after a song, "Hey, all right, man! That's really fine. Way to go!" He tried to soften Eno's hardness with relentless questions about bowings and techniques that the old man scorned to answer. One night he asked him, "You ever play the guitar?"

The old man stared blankly at Snipe for a moment, his lips moving in and out, then got up and laid his fiddle on the chair. He went into the back room off the kitchen, and they heard the metal snap of latches being undone. Eno came out with a guitar made of painted metal and on the back a picture of a Hawaiian hula dancer swaying beneath a coconut palm. "That," said old Eno, "is a resonator guitar that my Uncle Bell give me in 1942. That's the one we use when we work up a new song." He looked over at Nell, stroked the woman-shaped body of the guitar with his old man's hand, slid his finger under the strings and caressed the edge of the sound hole. Snipe felt some dark, unspoken words trembling in the room. He stretched out his hand for the instrument, but before he could touch it, Eno hustled it jealously into the back room. "I wouldn't take nothing on this earth for it," he said. When he came back to his fiddle, away they all went with "Fried Potatoes," fat Nell belting out "French fries, home fries, potato cakes, potato pies," but looking sidelong at Snipe—with complicity, he thought—as if she wanted to laugh with him at the old man's tin guitar.

That was the night he saw how the trick was done. It was Nell, not Eno, who controlled which songs they played, and the tunes, he saw, had all been arranged at some earlier time in unchanging sets of six or seven. If she began with "There Is a Stranger in My Room Tonight," there must follow "Frozen Roses," and then "Rain on the Roof Makes Me Lonely." But if she began with "Lost Girls" or "Grass Fire," different sets of songs followed. He noticed for the first time that she hummed a few notes of the key song in each set as a signal to the others of what was coming. In his back corner he had never caught it. It was Nell who was the master of the group, not Eno.

Snipe began to play to her, even when old Shirletta trampled his filigreed arpeggios with her steely tremolo and Ruby drowned his fine, silken harmonics with flaring chords. He knew she heard every note he sent her. Nell, who wrote the songs and melodies, Nell who wrung lyrics and music from her life as casually as water from a dishrag. Now, on the sepia-toned album cover in his mind Nell stood alone.

He began to write a song himself, about the cedars—"I am a Prisoner of Some Green Trees"—and practiced for hours. The tune was a little like "Clementine." Catherine would come home smelling of hamburgers and find him hunched over the guitar, reworking a tiny phrase with numbed fingers, the scotch bottle on the floor, his back bent in futile concentration. For it was obvious that he had reached some plateau of accomplishment, that despite the passionate practice (intended to keep him from looking for a job, said Catherine), his playing failed to become brilliant, his phrasing and intonation remained hesitant. Yet he continued to sing and bay. The two hours he spent in the Twilights' kitchen each Wednesday sending musical messages to a fat woman with whom he had never spoken were the only times he felt he was approaching some form of happiness.

He thrust his song at them one night. "I made up this song about some trees; like I really like them but they are keeping me from doing what I wanna with my life," he said, not looking at Eno, and sang directly to Nell. The Twilights got the hang of the song right away and came in one by one, and when Nell sang in harmony with him "tall treees are my jail bars" he felt it was one of his life's finest times. He wanted to play through the song again, but Eno pointed his bow at Nell in an abrupt slash and she took them into "The Fallen Fawn."

In late September the frosts began, shriveling the clumps of maidenhair fern but sparing the last spotted tiger lilies. The coarse, vivid green of summer dulled; the meadow grass lodged under the weight of the autumn rain. Catherine did not come home one night and Snipe knew she must have spent it with the new owner of Poochie's Grill, a grinner named Omar, who had changed the name of the restaurant to Omar's Oasis, put in four palms and a ceiling fan, and hung some of Catherine's brown weavings on the wall as though they were paintings.

Snipe had feelings of melancholy, noticed leaf veins, flakes of mica in rocks, extraordinarily fine hairs on plant stems. The smell of woodsmoke and damp earth made his eyes flood with reasonless tears. Late one afternoon he stood on the dock drinking scotch from the Mexican glass Catherine had brought back from the Acapulco vacation. He stared at a peculiar lenticular cloud. He could hear the sullen hum of a truck on the road beyond the lake. The truck's buzz, and a tinny, faraway chain saw, made Snipe feel in a rush of misery that he had hardly had an hour's true happiness. The chance for that had gone when he followed Catherine in false respect for imitation Peruvian weaving. He wanted fat Nell and the freedom of dirty sheets, wanted to sit in a broken chair and play music and not have to make a mark in the world. That night he lay awake listening to Catherine's snores blending with the dying whines of cicadas.

In the morning he waited until he heard Catherine slam the door and drive away with Omar. Then he rose, washed his hair and body, and dressed in clean clothes, wearing for the first time the black silk shirt she had given him for his birthday. He drove down the gravel road between the hemlocks and turned onto the Twilights' ruined track.

Nell was alone in the kitchen making jelly. Shirletta, she said, had gone to town with her sister's daughter to buy school clothes for the kids. Ruby and Eno were cutting firewood up in back. He could hear the chain saws in the maple sugar bush beyond the cornfields. The kitchen was flooded with the heavy, cloying perfume of blackberry jelly. Nell leaned her stomach against the sink and hummed. The jelly bag slumped flaccidly in a bowl like some excised organ from a slaughtered animal. There was crimson scum clotted in the sink where she had flung it, skimmed from the seething jelly in the kettle. Her hands were stained purple and a rose flush tinted her round, solid arms, the strong column of her neck. Her hair was wound up in shining thick braids. Jelly jars glittered the color of chambered pomegranates as they stood cooling on the table, translucent skins of wax hardening on the surface. The chain saws were as monotonous as the night cicadas.

Snipe came up behind her and wrapped his arms around her waist, pressed his sallow face against her hot back. She smelled of road dust, of goldenrod and crushed sweet blackberries; her humming voice vibrated in his ear. Far away in the woods there was a cadenced shout and the leafy, thrashing fall of a tree. The chain saws faded from hearing. A yellowjacket, intoxicated by the sweet, musky scent, flew clumsily around the kitchen. Snipe gathered up Nell's flowery dress hem as carefully as if he were picking up glass jackstraws.

Later, while he was still pressed against her, she said, "They're coming down from the woods." They stared together at the field where the men were bumping along through the uncut hay like a vaudeville team mocking drunkards. "Ruby's hurt," she said, pushing him away and turning to face the door. He smoothed himself and went over to stand beside the hot stove where the jelly burned.

They came in, Ruby grinning in a fixed way as though a set of vise grips had bolted his jaw. His left arm was wrapped in Eno's bloodstained shirt. There were flecks of bloody matter on his face, and he held the injured arm protectively across his chest. The thick, white hair on old Eno's chest and bulging belly was flattened and mussed like a deer bed in the orchard, the two dark nipples peeping out like plum-colored eyes. They went to the sink, Eno on one side, Ruby swaying in the center, and Nell with her dimpled hands cupping the elbow of the hurt arm.

Snipe felt his throat bind as Nell unwrapped the shirt and laid bare the injury. Drops of blood fell heavily into the sink, puddling with the jelly. Snipe could smell Eno's underarms, a sharp skunky odor that mixed with the reek of sex and sugared fruit. "Get them bandages they give us that time," said old Eno, and Nell went into the pantry. They heard her tear open paper. She and Eno leaned together as they bound the surgical pad to Ruby's wound with a thick roll of gauze. A small red flower bloomed on the snowy bandage. "Hold that arm up in the air," said Eno, hoisting Ruby's elbow.

Later, Snipe thought that he should have gotten away then, should have slipped out the door, rolled the car silently down the track, and raced for the protection of the cedars. Instead he said, "Shouldn't he have a tourniquet on that arm?" Eno turned to stare at him, to wonder a few seconds, then the old man's eyes went to Nell. Her head was bent, her eyes down, and she wrapped and wrapped the gauze.

"Not if I want to keep my goddamned hand," said Ruby in a rough, clenched voice, but the point of crisis had shifted from his wound to Snipe's presence and Nell's hidden face. A knowledge of what had happened in the kitchen mounted as steadily as rising floodwater. Ruby set his mouth in a sardonic grin, but old Eno's hands were trembling, and he gasped for breath as though he were the one who had been wounded.

"Eno!" cried Snipe in a panic, "I love your daughter!" and he knew that he did not. It had always been the truck in the weeds.

"Fool," said Ruby between his teeth, "she's his wife."

Snipe could hear the scorched jelly crackling in the kettle. He glanced at the door, and at once Eno came for him, his heavy farmer's hand crooked into pincers. "I'll get you," he cried, his eyes slitted with rage and his teeth bared like a dog's, "I'll get you."

Snipe ran, stumbling on the bloody shirt, skidding on the stone doorstep, breaking his fingernails on the car door handle, jamming his foot painfully between the accelerator and the brake, and then cursing and shaking as the vehicle crashed down the rocky track. "Goddamn hillbillies," he said to the rearview mirror.

He drove fifty miles to the big town in the next county and drank scotch at Bob's Bar, a plywood-paneled hole with imitation Tiffany lampshades made of plastic. The raw red and blue colors hurt his eyes and gave him a headache. When someone put Willy Nelson on the antique jukebox, he left. He wanted to hear Haydn. Haydn seemed safe and alluring like a freshly made bed with plump white pillows and a silken comforter. He could sink into Haydn.

He bought a symphony on tape at the discount drugstore, then hit the shopping mall for all of Catherine's favorites, the champagne, lobster, hearts of endive, a Black Forest cake, and Viennese coffee with cinnamon. It came to more than a hundred dollars and he wrote bad checks with the sure feeling that he and Catherine would make a lucky new start. He was all through with the Twilights. When she got home he would have everything ready, fireplace lit, fresh sheets, chilled champagne glasses. He was suffused with mounting nervousness like a bird before a storm, and went again and again through the long afternoon to the end of the dock to stand and stare across the water, longing for Catherine's two hundred fragile bones and her shallow flesh. When a dead branch fell from one of the cedars, he dragged it eagerly to the moldering pile behind the garage.

It was easy. She came back to him willingly, ready to play their old games. They made fun of Omar's restaurant hands, and Snipe said the country music thing wasn't working out. There were other things they could do, maybe go out west, New Mexico or Arizona. Snipe knew somebody would pay him good money to collect the wild seed of jimsonweed.

They lay in the pillows in the corner of the sofa, Snipe's fingers sliding automatically up and down her arm, the rough calluses rasping on the silk. After a while Haydn's precise measures were like faded pencil drawings on thin paper. The champagne bottle was empty. Catherine rolled passionately against him, and with the dry feeling that he was saying catechism he rested his mouth against the beat of her heart. He thought how it would be out west with the flat, sepia-tinted earth and the immense sky of a hard, lonely blue. Out there the roads stretched forever to the horizon. Snipe saw himself alone, driving a battered old truck through the shimmering heat, the wind booming through the open windows. The windshield was starred with a bullet hole. He wore scuffed cowboy boots, faded jeans, and a torn black shirt with a cactus embroidered on the back, and the heel of his hand beat out a Tex-Mex rhythm on the cracked steering wheel.

The Unclouded
Day

IT was a rare thing, a dry, warm spring that swelled into summer so ripe and full that gleaming seed bent the grass low a month before its time; a good year for grouse. When the season opened halfway through September, the heat of summer still held, dust lay like yellow flour on the roads, and a perfume of decay came from the thorned mazes where blackberries fell and rotted on the ground. Grouse were in the briars, along the watercourses, and, drunk on fermenting autumn juices, they flew recklessly, their wings cleaving the shimmering heat of the day.

Santee did not care to hunt birds in such high-colored weather. Salty sweat stung the whipped-branch welts on his neck and arms, the dog worked badly and the birds spoiled in an hour. In their sour, hot intestines he smelled imminent putrefaction. The feathers stuck to his hands, for Earl never helped gut them. Noah, the dog, lay panting in the shade.

The heat wave wouldn't break. Santee longed for the cold weather and unclouded days that lay somewhere ahead, for the sharp chill of spruce shadow, icy rime thickening over osier twigs and a hard autumnal sky cut by the parabolic flights of birds in the same way pond ice was cut by skaters. Ah goddamn, thought Santee, there were better things to do than hunt partridge with a fool in these burning days.

Earl had come to Santee the year before and begged him to teach him how to hunt birds. He had a good gun, he said, a Tobias Hume. Santee thought it overrated and overpriced, but it was a finer instrument than his own field-grade Jorken with the cracked stock he'd meant to replace for years. (The rough walnut blank lay on the workbench out in the barn, cans of motor oil and paint standing on it; the kids had ruined the checkering files by picking out butternut meats with them.) Santee's gun, like its owner, was inelegant and long in the tooth, but it worked well.

Earl had come driving up through the woods to Santee's place, overlooking the mess in the yard, nodding to Verna, and he had flattered Santee right out of his mind.

"Santee," he said, measuring him, seeing how he was inclined, "I've talked to people around and they say you're a pretty good hunter. I want to learn how to hunt birds. I want you to teach me. I'll pay you to teach me everything about them."

Santee could see that Earl had money. He wore nice boots, rich corduroy trousers in a golden syrup color, his hands were shaped like doves and his voice rolled out of his throat like sweet batter. He was not more than thirty, Santee thought, looking at the firm cheek slabs and thick yellow hair.

"I usually hunt birds by myself. Or with my boys." Santee gave each word its fair measure of weight. "Me'n the dog." Noah, lying on the porch under the rusty glider, raised his head at the sound of "birds" and watched them.

"Nice dog," said Earl in his confectionary voice. Santee folded his arms across his chest rather than let them hang by his sides. Hands in the pockets was even worse, he thought, looking at Earl, a wastrel's posture.

Earl oiled Santee with his voice. "All I ask, Santee, is that you try it two or three times, and if you don't want to continue, why then, I'll pay for your time." He gave Santee a smile, the leaf-colored eyes under the gleaming lids shifting from Santee to the warped screen door, to the scabby paint on the clapboards, to the run-down yard. Santee looked off to the side as though the muscles in his own eyes were weak.

"Maybe give it a try. Rather go on a weekday than a weekend. You get away on Monday?"

Earl could get away any day Santee wanted. He worked at home.

"What doin'?" asked Santee, letting his arms hang down.

"Consulting. I analyze stocks and economic trends." Santee saw that Earl was younger than his own oldest son, Derwin, whose teeth were entirely gone and who worked up at the veneer mill at Potumsic Falls breathing fumes and tending a machine with whirling, curved blades. Santee said he would go out with Earl on Monday. He didn't know how to say no.

The first morning was a good one, a solid bright day with a spicy taste to the air. Noah was on his mettle, eager to find birds and showing off a little for the stranger. Santee set Earl some distance away on his right until he could see how he shot.

Noah worked close. He stiffened two yards away from birds in front, he pointed birds to the left, the right. A single step from Santee or Earl sent partridge bursting out of the cover and into straightaway flight. He pinned them in trees and bushes, scented them feeding on fallen fruit or dusting in powdery bowls of fine earth, marked them as they pattered through wood sorrel. He worked like two dogs, his white sides gliding through the grass, his points so rigid he might have been a glass animal. The grouse tore up the air and the shotguns bellowed. Earl, Santee saw, didn't know enough to say "Nice dog" when it counted.

Santee held himself back in order to let his pupil learn, but Earl was a slow, poor shot. The bird would be fifty yards out and darting through safe holes in the air when he finally got the gun around and pulled the trigger. Sometimes a nervous second bird would go up before Earl fired at the first one. He couldn't seem to catch the rhythm, and had excuses for each miss.

"Caught the butt end in my shirt pocket flap," he'd say, laughing a little, and, "My fingers are stiff from carrying the gun," and, "Oh, that one was gone before I could get the bead on him."

Santee tried over and over again to show him that you didn't aim at the bird, that you just threw up the gun and fired in the right place.

"You have to shoot where they're goin', not where they are." He made Earl watch him on the next one, how the gun notched into place on his shoulder, how his right elbow lifted smoothly as his eyes bent toward the empty air the bird was about to enter. *Done!* went the shotgun, and the bird fell like a nut.

"Now you do it," said Santee.

But when a grouse blustered out of the wild rose haws, Earl only got the gun to his hip, then twisted his body in an odd backward contortion as he fired. The train of shot cut a hole in the side of a tamarack and the bird melted away through the trees.

"I'n see you need a lot of practice," said Santee.

"What I need *is* practice," agreed Earl, "and that is what I am paying for."

"Try movin' the stock up to your shoulder," said Santee, thinking that his kids had shot better when they were eight years old.

They worked through the morning, Santee illustrating swift reaction and tidy speed, and Earl sweating and jerking like an old Vitagraph film, trying to line up the shotgun with the bird. Santee shot seven grouse and gave four to Earl who had missed every one. Earl gave Santee a hundred dollars and said he wanted to do it again.

"I can practice all the rest of this week," he said, making it sound like a piano lesson.

The next three Mondays were the same. They went out and worked birds. Earl kept shooting from the hip. With his legs spraddled out he looked like an old-time gangster spraying the rival mob with lead.

"Listen here," said Santee, "there are six more weeks left in the season, which means we go out six more times. Now, I am not after more money, but you might want to think about goin' out a little more often." Earl was eager and said he'd pay.

"Three times a week. I can go Monday, Wednesday and Friday." They tried it that way. Then they tried Monday, Tuesday and Wednesday for continuity. Earl was paying Santee three hundred dollars a week and he hadn't shot a single bird.

"How's about this?" said Santee, feeling more and more like a cheating old whore every time they went out. "How's about I come over to your place on the weekend with a box of clay pigeons and you practice shootin' them up? No charge! Just to sort of get your eye in, and the gun up to your shoulder."

"Yes, but I'm not upset about missing the birds, you know," said Earl, looking in the trees. "I've read the books and I know it takes years before you develop that fluid, almost instinctive response to the grouse's rising thunder. I know, believe me, how difficult a target these speedy fliers really are, and I'm willing to work on it, even if it takes years."

Santee had not heard shooting birds was that hard, but he knew Earl was no good; he had the reflexes of a snowman. He said to Verna, "That Earl has got to get it together or I can't keep takin' his money. I feel like I'm goin' to the salt mines every time we go out. I don't have the heart to hunt any more on my own, out of fear I'll bust up a bunch of birds he needs for practice. Dammit, all the fun is goin' out of it."

"The money is good," said Verna, giving the porch floor a shove that set the glider squeaking. Her apron was folded across her lap, her arms folded elbow over elbow with her hands on her shoulders, her ankles crossed against the coolness of the night. She wore the blue acrylic slippers Santee had given her for Mother's Day.

"I just wonder how I got into it," he said, closing his eyes and gliding.

Santee bought a box of a hundred clay pigeons and drove up to Earl's house on a Sunday afternoon. It was the kind of day people decided to go for a ride.

"I wish I hadn't come," said Verna, looking through the cloudy windshield at Earl's home, an enormous Swiss chalet with windows like tan bubbles in the roof and molded polystyrene pillars holding up a portico roof. She wouldn't get out of the truck, but sat for two hours with the window ground up. Santee knew how she felt, but he had to go. He was hired to teach Earl how to shoot birds.

🐦 🐦 🐦

There was a big porch and on it was Earl's wife, as thin as a folded dollar bill, her hand as narrow and cold as a trout. A baby crawled around inside a green plastic-mesh pen playing with a tomato. Earl told them to watch.

"Watch Daddy shoot the birdy!" he said.

"Beady!" said the baby.

"Knock those beadies dead, Earl," said the wife, drawing her fingernail through a drop of moisture that had fallen from her drink onto the chair arm.

Santee cocked his arm back again and again and sent the clay discs flying out over a garden of dark shrubs. His ears rang. The baby screamed every time the gun went off, but Earl wouldn't let the woman take him inside.

"Watch!" he cried. "Dammit, watch Daddy shoot the beady!" He would get the gun to his hip and bend his back into the strange posture he had made his trademark. Him and Al Capone, thought Santee, saying, "Put it to your shoulder," like a broken record. "It won't backfire."

He looked to see if Earl shut his eyes behind the yellow spectacles when he pulled the trigger, but couldn't tell. After a long time a clay round flew into three black pieces and Earl shrieked, "I got it!" as if it were a wooly mammoth. It was the first object he had hit since Santee had met him.

"Pretty good," he lied. "*Now* you're doin' it."

Verna called all the kids home for dinner a week later. There was home-cured ham basted with Santee's hard cider, baked Hubbard squash, mashed potato with Jersey cream spattered over each mound and a platter of roast partridge glazed with chokecherry jelly.

Before they sat down at the table Verna got everybody out in the yard to clean it up. They all counted one-two-three and heaved the carcass of Santee's 1952 Chevrolet in with the torn chicken wire, rotted fence posts and dimpled oil cans. Derwin drove the load to the dump after dinner and brought back a new lawn mower Verna had told him to get.

The next day she waded the brook, feeling for spherical stones of a certain size with her feet. Santee carried them up to the house in a grain bag. When they had dried on the porch she painted them snow white and set them in a line along the driveway. Santee saw the beauty of it—the green shorn grass, the gleaming white stones. It all had something to do with teaching Earl how to hunt, but aside from the money he didn't know what.

After a while he did. It was that she wouldn't let him quit. She would go out into the yard at the earliest light of hunting days— Santee had come to think of them as work days—walking in the wet grass and squinting at the sky to interpret the character of the new day. She got back into bed and put her cold feet on Santee's calves.

"It's cloudy," she would say. "Rain by noon." Santee would groan, because Earl did not like to get his gun wet.

"Won't it hurt it?" Earl always asked, as though he knew it would.

"Don't be no summer soldier," said Santee. "Wipe it down when you get back home and put some WD-40 to it, all good as new." It took him a while to understand that it wasn't the gun. Earl didn't like to get rain down his neck or onto his shooting glasses with the yellow lenses, didn't care to feel the cold drops trace narrow trails down his back and forearms, nor to taste the salty stuff that trickled from his hatband to the corners of his mouth.

They were walking through the deep wet grass, the rain drumming hard enough to make the curved blades bounce up and down. Earl's wet twill pants were plastered to him like blistered skin. Something in the way he pulled at the sodden cloth with an arched finger and thumb told Santee he was angry at the rain, at Santee, maybe mad enough to quit shelling out three hundred dollars a week for no birds and a wet nature walk. Good, thought Santee.

But the rain stopped and a watery sun warmed their backs. Noah found tendrils of rich hot grouse scent lying on the moist air as solidly as cucumber vines on the garden earth. He locked into his catatonic point again and again, and they sent the birds flying in arcs of shaken raindrops. Earl didn't connect, but he said he knew it took years before shooters got the hang of it.

The only thing he shot that season was the clay pigeon, and the year ended with no birds for Earl, money in Santee's bank account and a row of white stones under the drifting snow. Santee thought it was all over, a bad year to be buried with the memory of other bad years.

Through the next spring and summer he never thought of Earl without a shudder. The droughty grouse summer held into September. Santee bored the replacement stock for the Jorken. He bought a new checkering file and sat on the porch after dinner making a good job of it and waiting for the heat to break, thinking about going out by himself in the chill October days as the woods and fields faded and clods of earth froze hard. He hunched toward the west on the steps, catching the last of the good light; the days were getting shorter in spite of the lingering heat from the baked earth. Verna fanned her damp neck with a sale flier that had come in the mail.

"Car's comin'," she said. Santee stopped rasping and listened.

"It's that Earl again," said Verna, recognizing the Saab before it was in sight.

He was a little slicker in his talk, and wore an expensive game vest with a rubber pocket in the back where the birds would lie, their dark blood seeping into the seams.

"My wife gave me this," he said, and he showed them the new leather case for his shotgun, stamped with his initials and a design of three flying grouse.

"No," Santee tried to say, "I've taught you all I can. I don't want to take your money no more." But Earl wasn't going to let him go. Now he wanted a companion with a dog and Santee was it, with no pay.

"After all, we got to know each other very well last year. We're a good team—friends," Earl said, looking at the fresh paint on the clapboards. "Nice job," he said.

Santee went because he had taken Earl's money. Until the fool shot a bird on his own or gave up, Santee was obliged to keep going out with him. The idea that Earl might ruin every fall for the rest of his life made Santee sick.

"I've come to hate partridge huntin'," he told Verna in the sultry night. "I hate those white stones, too." She knew what he was talking about.

Derwin heard Earl bragging down at the store, some clam dip and a box of Triscuits in front of him on the counter. Earl's new game vest hung open casually, his yellow shooting glasses dangled outside the breast pocket, one earpiece tucked in through the buttonhole.

"Yes," he said, "we did quite well today. Limited out. I hunt with Santee, you know—grand old fellow."

"He didn't know who I was," raged Derwin, who had wanted to say something deadly but hadn't found any words until he drove up home and sat on the edge of the porch. "Whyn't you tell him where to head in, Pa? At least quit givin' him birds he makes like he shot hisself."

"I wish I could," groaned Santee. "If he would just get one bird I could cut loose, or if he decided to go in for somethin' else and quit comin' around. But I feel like I owe him part of a bargain. I took a lot of his money and all he got out of it was a clay pigeon."

"You don't owe him nothin'," said Derwin.

Earl came up again the next morning. He parked his Saab in the shade and beeped the horn in Santee's truck until he came out on the porch.

"Where you want to hit today?" called Earl. It wasn't a question. In some way he'd gotten ahead of Santee. "Might as well take your truck, it's already scratched up. Maybe go to the Africa covert and then hit White Birch Heaven."

Earl had given fanciful names to the different places they hunted. "Africa" because there was long yellow grass on the edge of a field Earl said looked like the veldt. "White Birch Heaven" because Noah had pointed six birds in twenty minutes. Santee had taken two, leaving the rest for seed after Earl shot the tops out of the birches. They were grey birches, but Santee had not cared enough to say so, any more than he pointed out that the place had been called "Ayer's high pasture" for generations.

It was breathlessly close as they climbed toward the upper fields of the old farm. The sky was a slick white color. Noah lagged, the dust filling his nose. Santee's shirt was wet and he could hear thunder in the ground, the storm that had been building for weeks of drumming heat. Deerflies and gnats bit furiously at their ears and necks.

"Gonna be a hell of a storm," said Santee.

Nothing moved. They might have been in a painted field, walking slowly across the fixed landscape where no bird could ever fly, nor tree fall. The leaves hung limp, soil crumbled under their feet.

"You won't put no birds up in this weather," said Santee.

"What?" asked Earl, the yellow glasses shining like insect eyes.

"I said, it's gonna be a corker of a storm. See there?" Santee dropped his arm toward the west where a dark humped line illuminated by veins of lightning lay across the horizon. "Comin' right for us like a house on fire. Time to go home and try again another day."

He started back down, paying no attention to Earl's remarks that the storm was a long way off and there were birds up there. He was dogged enough, thought Santee sourly.

As they went down the hill, slipping on the drought-polished grass, the light thickened to a dirty ocher. Little puffs of wind raised dust and started the poplars vibrating.

"You might be right," said Earl, passing Santee. "It's coming along pretty fast. I just felt a drop."

❦ ❦ ❦

Santee looked back over his shoulder and saw the black wall of cloud swelling into the sky. Bursts of wind ripped across the slope and the rolling grind of thunder shook the earth. Noah scampered fearfully, his tail clamped between his legs, his eyes seeking Santee's again and again.

"We're goin', boy," said Santee encouragingly.

The first raindrops hit like bird shot, rattling down on them and striking the trees with flat smacks. White hail pellets bounced and stung where they hit flesh. They ran into a belt of spruce where there was a narrow opening in the trees like a bowling alley. Halfway down its length a panicky grouse flew straight away from them. It was at least eighty yards out, an impossible distance, when Earl heaved his shotgun onto his hip and fired. As he pulled the trigger, lightning struck behind them. The grouse dropped low and skimmed away, but Earl believed he had hit it. Buried in the sound of his crashing gun he had not even heard the lightning strike.

"Get it!" he shouted at Noah, who had pasted himself to Santee's legs when the lightning cracked the spruce. "Make your dog get it!" yelled Earl, pointing in the direction the grouse had flown. The rain roared down on them. Earl ran for evergreen shelter in the direction his bird had vanished, still pointing through the bursting rain. "Fetch! Fetch! Oh, you damn thing, fetch my bird!"

Santee, trusting the principle that lightning never strikes twice in the same place, went under the smoking spruce. The bolt had entered the pith and exploded the heartwood in a column of live steam. White wood welled out of the riven bark. Almost at his feet, lying where they had fallen from the needled canopy of the top branches, were three dead grouse. They steamed gently in the cold rain. The hard drops struck the breast feathers like irregular heartbeats. Santee picked them up and looked at them. He turned them around and upside down. As soon as the rain slackened he pulled his shirt up over his head and made a run for Earl's tree.

"You don't need to yell at my dog. Here's your birds. Three in one shot, mister man, is somethin' I never seen before. You sure have learned how to shoot." He shook his head.

Earl's eyes were hidden behind the rain-streaked yellow shooting glasses. His thick cheeks were wet and his lips flapped silently. "Something felt right," he gabbled, seizing the birds. "I knew something was going to happen today. I guess I was ready for the big breakthrough."

He talked all the way back to Santee's truck, and as they drove through the woods, the windshield wipers beating, the damp air in the cab redolent of wet dog, explained how he'd felt the birds were there, how he'd felt the gun fall into line on them, how he saw the feathers fountain up.

"I saw right where they went down," he said. Santee thought he probably believed he had. "But that dog of yours . . ."

Santee pulled up in his yard beside Earl's Saab and set the hand brake. The rain flowed over the windshield in sheets. Santee cleared his throat.

"This is the parting of our ways," he said. "I can take a good deal, but I won't have my dog called down."

Earl smirked; he knew Santee was jealous. "That's okay with me," he said, and ran through the hammering rain to his car, squeezing the grouse in his arms.

Santee woke before dawn, jammed up against Verna. He could see the pale mist of breath floating from her nostrils. Icy air flowed through an inch of open window. He slipped out of bed to close it, saw the storm had cleared the weather. Stars glinted like chips of mica in the paling sky, hoarfrost coated the fields and the row of stones along the drive. The puddles in the road were frozen solid. It was going to be a cold, unclouded day. He laughed to himself as he got back into the warm bed, wondering what Earl had said when he plucked three partridges that were already cooked.

In the Pit

"BLUE," said his mother, looking like Charles Laughton in a flowered wrapper, "won't you do this one little thing for me?" She tapped her cigarette ash into a ceramic sombrero on the dinette table. Papers, magazines, letters, bills, offers to develop her film in twenty-four hours or insure her credit cards against loss, fliers and folders spilled around her. Her white hair was rumpled like a cloud torn by wind, her eyes the common pastel of greeting-card rabbits. Blue looked away from the heavy sleeves of flesh that hung from her upper arms, from the smoke curling out of her nose.

"Now. It's in here somewhere, and full of spelling mistakes." She shuffled a deck of envelopes. "Here, sheriff writes blah, blah, vandals broke in. Threw chairs and furniture over the ledge, smashed dishes, broke windows, and they don't know who did it." The letter grated across spilled sugar as she slid it under her coffee cup.

"You could drive up in a couple of hours, Blue, see how bad it is, put on a lock or whatever. Revisit the scenes of your childhood," she said, puffing her mocking voice out with the smoke, "those happy hours you spent in the loft while your father and I shouted at each other."

He remembered the neatness of the camp, the moon-blonde kitchen with its silvery pots and pans on hooks, the blue shutters, the narrow clenched spirals of the braided rug, so different from this apartment where his mother's carnival-tent clothes hung on the chairs and shoes sprawled like dead fish. She saw his look.

❧ ❧ ❧

"I don't know how I did it in those days, keeping everything cleansy-weansy, always bent over that damn little sink the size of a sardine tin. Honey, I don't know how I did it." She threw a few envelopes into the air and let them fall in disorder.

"You're a wild woman, mother," he said.

Blue was visiting to show photographs of his wife, Grace, and their adopted daughter, Bonnie. The pool, little Bonnie and her pony, even Grace's richly colored hair and nails demonstrated his success after years of failed starts at one thing and another. Blue had made his life over, had repaired himself through a class in Assertiveness Training, had learned how to look into others' eyes, to clasp their hands firmly, to bend them to his will. He had dieted eighteen pounds away through willpower and dressed his new shape with style. A dark, wavy hairpiece gave his fleshy face with its long sheep's mouth a kind of springing vigor.

He had two weeks for everything, the travel, the photographs, the overhaul of memories. This was the first time he had seen his mother since the funeral in Las Cruces seven years earlier. She had arrived late from the airport in a mocha-colored limousine, accompanied by an unknown man wearing saddle oxfords. After the service she had come up to Blue, embraced him and said, "Thank god that's over, but your father would have loved it." She had climbed back into the limousine and waved goodbye. Grace stood beside him, stiff as a curtain rod, insulted because she had not been introduced.

Besides the photographs Blue brought his mother an armful of gentians, the deep emotional color of ocean beyond the sight of land. She put them in a jar of water with an aspirin to revive them, but they had traveled too far; the stems bent weakly, the rich petals furled and closed. At least he had brought them.

That night he tried to sleep on the sofa, but the reek of an ashtray gave him a headache. His body was still thrumming with the vibrations of flight. There were things about the apartment he didn't like: a pair of long black rubbers on the floor of the hall closet, the copies of *Boxing Roundup* on top of the toilet tank, the coffee mug stenciled "Lover Man" in the cupboard. He carried the ashtray to the kitchen to empty it. Not quietly enough; she came padding in, as big as a rolled mattress.

"Well, look at that," she said, and the color of her voice was one she used to reserve for his father.

In the morning mirror he looked purposeful again, and proved it by making the breakfast. He cleaned the stove, wiped the counters while she was in the bathroom. They ate together at the formica table, honey-thick sunlight flowing across the surface, the toast crumbs casting shadows as long as pencils. "I could go up to the camp," he said. He smiled without showing his teeth. The idea of the camp, of getting away from the dead gentians and the mug in the cupboard was a good one.

"I hope I never have to go up there again. Blue." She looked at him as if he were a fortune-teller who had already pocketed the fee. "Blue, look the place over and see what you think it'd bring on the market. There's three acres goes with it."

He rented a sleeping bag and snowshoes, bought toilet paper and kerosene, matches and cans of Dinty Moore beef stew.

"For the Lord's sake," she said in her biting voice, "they have stores up there, you know. It's not Darkest Africa." But he showed her how he did things in a careful way, packed the car with the heavy objects at the bottom.

He pulled onto the track to the camp in late afternoon, shadows pouring out of the spruce like dark water, and as he knelt on the snow to buckle the snowshoe straps, his eye caught a flickering, circular motion out on the main road. A tall shape canted at an angle, a black figure that seemed to balance on a thin rod, bent into the curve and became a man on a bicycle, knees doggedly rising and falling like the oars of a solitary rowing.

The bicycle drew near, and Blue saw fallen cheeks stubbled with white, the ears red and twisted as if they had been boiled. The rider mounted the hill and came up against the sky like a weathervane whose ingenious wheels turned in the wind. One slow, bare hand raised a paper bag to the mouth, then the rider disappeared over the hill as if he were sinking into tar.

One of those old boys. Blue knew that kind, pumping along

on a kid's bike with its fat tires and faded handlebar streamers, face blazing with drink and the abrasive wind thrown off by passing cars.

He was astonished to come on the camp in a quarter of an hour. When he was a child it had seemed deep in the woods, a remote place that could be reached only after a difficult journey through dark tunnels of trees. Now, in the light reflected off the snow, the place had a bruised look as though it had been dragged through hard times on the end of a dirty rope. The trees were scrubby spruce and fir. Everything seemed smaller, less exalted.

Inside the camp he smelled the mournful odor of trodden cloves. There was the brown sofa that folded out into a bed, the fireplace with a little pile of soot and a dead bird in it. There had always been a dead bird in the fireplace when they opened the camp. He threw it out into the soundless snow.

He climbed the stair to the loft that was his old room. The husks of dead flies, their legs as rigid as waxed threads, strewed the windowsills; a bright, buffy dusk bloomed in the dusty panes. His old cot stood under the west window as it always had. This raw place had been his first solitude, and the unfinishedness of the room had matched his child's belief that he could become anything. Now clouds of frosty breath poured from his mouth like the wraiths of unspoken declarations, and he went back down the stairs.

In the kitchen he unpacked his supplies. There was only one chair and he wondered what had happened to the others. The cloves and peppercorns spilled by the vandals broke underfoot like hard-backed beetles. He swept up the painted buds from the smashed plates, a round cup handle that lay like a china monocle over a staring knothole in the floor. As the flame seized the blackened lamp wick a yellow glow like a sense of well-being rose up the walls and there was the smell of burning dust and hot metal.

The next morning he awakened in ringing silence. The hairpiece lay like a sleeping marmot on top of his folded clothes. His feet recognized the familiar floorboards and in the kitchen, cool, pure light flowed over his hands like water. He heated stew in the can and ate pale bread, for there were no pots and pans, no toaster.

Outside he studied the camp, the stains, the cracks, the curling shingles. He could make these faults over. He would come back in the summer with Grace and Bonnie. Bonnie would sleep on the cot in the loft. He wrote a list of what must be done in the notebook that was always in his shirt pocket.

There was a small cliff behind the camp. He walked to the edge and looked down at chair legs sticking out of the snow, the curve of a griddle like a black rising moon. The forks and knives had all disappeared down narrow, deep holes, like silvery snakes.

It was the morning's work to drag the snow in the pit with a garden rake, discovering piepans, the old dead dog's dish, a pair of sugar tongs. The holes he made in the depths of the snow were a deep, unearthly blue. The rake snagged a rusted quart milk can, and as he knocked the snow from it, a double image sailed into his mind like a pair of pirate ships: the man on the bicycle—Mr. Fitzroy holding the milk can.

In those childhood days his father had driven down to Fitzroy's barn every evening for sweet milk dipped from the tank, the shuddering liquid releasing a smell of torn grass and rain. Mr. Fitzroy handed the can to Blue. A tight metal cap fit over the neck and as the metal chilled a fine silvery dew formed; in it he traced his evanescent name with his fingernail, drew pictures of mountains and flags and the triangular faces of cats.

Mr. Fitzroy washed his hands by darting them into the stream of scalding water that gushed out of the milk room spigot. After the milking was done he sat beside his wife on the porch and played "Lady of Spain" on the accordion. Mrs. Fitzroy cut and whittled. There were her wooden animals on the windowsills, a dog with a curved tail, a figure with an unfinished face. At night the light quivered behind them and they seemed to shrink from the assaults of moths on the glass. Blue and his father listened, sitting in the car with the windows down and slapping mosquitoes with a sound like sparse applause.

Blue guessed now that the old lady had died, and Mr. Fitzroy gone down to the bottle.

He made his list: get the electricity turned on, call Grace in Las Cruces, three panes of glass, glazing compound, scouring powder, sponges, Murphy's Oil Soap, a new broom, hooks to rehang the pots and pans. The festering, cracked linoleum around the sink caught his eye and he wrote "tiles, adhesive, trowel." There was time enough to do these things.

On the main highway the resentful landscape showed itself to him, a stiff, hard country with rigid trees, frost-shattered masses of rock and shadowy gorges. The road to the shopping mall in Canker looped and doubled like intestine, ran between a stream and the leaning cliffs. Ravens flew up from crushed mats of fur and gristle at the rushing approach of his car, and dropped again before he was out of sight. The sky was filled with raw, bunched clouds. He crossed a bridge where a bicycle leaned against the guardrail like a tired animal.

Mr. Fitzroy, wearing old-fashioned overalls with wide, simple legs, was a mile farther on, his hand uplifted at the sound of Blue's car. Blue stopped and opened the door.

"Hello, Mr. Fitzroy. What's wrong with your bicycle?"

"Nothin'. Always hitch this part. Steep hills." He was not surprised at being named by an apparent stranger, didn't look at Blue, but stared fixedly down the highway in the direction of the shopping mall like a compass needle straining toward the north. They rode in silence. At the shopping mall Blue said, "I'm going back up to the camp in an hour. If you want a ride, I'll leave the door unlocked." The old man mumbled, "Obliged," and headed for the revolving "Harry's Bottle-O-Rama" sign.

It was much more than an hour. The New Mexico call was a long one. Everyone missed him, said Grace, but she heated up when he told her not to send the special drawings Bonnie was making for "Gramma."

"She isn't very grandmotherly, Grace." He didn't say the photographs were still in his suitcase, that his mother hadn't seen the color prints of Bonnie in her little yellow bathing suit, of Bonnie on the spotted pony. He didn't mention the cup on his mother's shelf, talked instead about repairing the camp.

"What kind of camp is it?" She seemed to be picturing Boy Scouts and sing-alongs.

"Our old camp, where we used to go in the summers." The tough edge in Grace's voice kept him from saying they could use the camp in the summers.

"It seems funny," said Grace, "to go way back east just to fix an old camp for a woman who doesn't seem to care about her only grandchild." She put Bonnie on the line. Blue promised to bring her two presents.

"I like it when you're gone," said Bonnie, "because we have fried chicken every night."

"Well, I have Dinty Moore stew," he said, and the last thing he heard, after Grace said goodbye, was Bonnie screaming for dinty soup.

He made his way back to the car through the frozen grocery carts that stood scattered across the lot like beasts on the winter prairie. A heavy cold descended as though some hand had cranked the mottled sky down on bent figures in quilted coats and shuffling foam boots.

"God, I about give up on you," said Mr. Fitzroy, each word afloat on curling fumes of liquor. Blue started the car, thinking that if he struck a match there would be a flash fire. It was only a little past four, but twilight fell hard into darkness before the lights of the shopping center disappeared behind them.

"You look like I ought to know your name, but I forget it," said Mr. Fitzroy. Blue said his name, reminded him of the milk can and the accordion, mentioned Mrs. Fitzroy in the sad voice he reserved for speaking of the sick and dying. "I remember she used to carve figures."

"You don't know the half of it," said the old man. He took a carton of orange juice from the bag at his feet and poured some into a half-empty whiskey bottle, shook the bottle gently and offered it to Blue, then drank himself.

"I'm livin' down in the milk room these days," he said. "The house burned couple years back, seemed like the milk room was good enough. Cows gone, sleep late, watch the television, take it easy for a while, and you know what, I got sick of it. People here are no good, all these new people from down below always goin' off the road and want you to pull them out for nothin' with the tractor. Think it runs on prune juice. Think if you got a tractor you're dyin' to get out there and pull people out of the ditch."

He shook the mixture in the bottle until it frothed, and drank. "The accordion got burned up in the fire. I'm surprised you remember that. But I wish that milk room was bigger. I got pretty steady company now. I see on the teevee they want a place to stay for these fellas just got out of prison and no place to go. I write them a letter, say what I got ain't much, but I'm willin' to share it." His voice strengthened with self-appreciation. "See, I'm not one of them that holds a man's past against him. Anyway, they leave it up to the fella that's gettin' out if he wants to try it. I've had a few stay. Got one there now, Gilbert, him and me get along pretty good." He looked at Blue out of the corners of his veined eyes. "I don't hold the past against nobody."

Blue stopped at the bridge where Mr. Fitzroy's bicycle still leaned on the rail. He hoisted it into the trunk and tied the lid down with a stretch cord.

"What I want to do," said Mr. Fitzroy, moving the bottle gently in a circle so the liquid inside formed a whirlpool, "is sell my place and get out of here. Me and Gilbert want to go out west and pan for gold. Look at this." He struggled to get his wallet out of his pocket, opened the glove compartment, and by its tiny light, searched until he found a bit of paper. Blue saw the words "YOUR OWN LAND IN COLORADO $39.50 PER MONTH."

Mr. Fitzroy leaned close to the paper and recited with the smoothness of a hundred readings, " 'No down payment, no interest, your own spread on Wild Buffalo Mesa. Get away from it

all. Come to the big sky country where wild horses roam free
among the sagebrush and breathe the unspoiled air.' "

"What do you get for water rights?" asked Blue.

"Water rights! Just drill a deep well if you got to, or find a
fresh spring. Track them wild horses, see where they drink, and
that's your water."

"Um," said Blue, thinking of the parched, pale land and the
tufts of bunchgrass spaced far apart like the repeated pattern on
wallpaper, the place where land without water was worthless,
and there was a lot of worthless land.

Light was shining out of the milk room window, and Mr.
Fitzroy went in, leaving the door open, while Blue pulled the bicycle free.

"Come in and say howdy to my partner," shouted the old man.

The big stainless steel tank was gone, replaced by odd pieces
of furniture, a frowsty bed, a table with bulbous legs. On the
table in a welter of newspapers, beer cans and dirty plates was a
gleaming toaster with a fleur-de-lis design on its side, and he
knew it immediately. It was their old toaster from the camp.

Once he had tried to grill a cheese sandwich in that toaster
and the bread caught fire, black smoke as though from burning
tires billowed out of the chrome. His parents shouted. His
mother flapped the air with a towel and screamed, "You damn
little fool to try to make a sandwich in a toaster!" and his father
hurled words like clods of dirt. "What do you expect, the kid has
never seen any kind of food fixed except cornflakes and canned
soup." She threw the toaster as hard as she could, and his father
caught it, hot and smoking, strings of cheese looping across the
floor. Blue ran up to the loft where he cried for the cheese sandwich as though it were the last one in the world, and the shouting below went on and on, and then the brown sofa creaked as
though they were tearing it apart. The next day his father's hands
were bandaged, but the toaster still worked and they had kept on
using it.

"Meet Gilbert," said Mr. Fitzroy. The lamp was behind the

seated figure and he seemed, for a minute, to be edged in a rim of fire, with round eyeglasses glinting like circles of steel. Then Gilbert teetered on his chair legs and looked to the side. His crimpy, tan hair was arranged in three large standing waves across the top of his head. His face was the color of a cracker, as stiff as if it had been baked, his eyes like a hen's, yellow and ignorant.

Gilbert put out a limp, hot hand. He was wearing fancy cowboy boots with bright green heels, probably the first things he had bought when he got out of prison. Blue knew how to size up failures like Gilbert in a minute.

"What took you so long," said Gilbert in a rattling, tinny voice to Mr. Fitzroy. "I got no bike or car so I'm just suppose to sit here and wait, whatever you want to do is suppose to be fine."

Mr. Fitzroy's voice was gentle. "Don't make a fuss, because I'm back now. How about a nice little beer?" Gilbert put out his hand for the foaming can. The old man held another up for Blue, but he said he had to go. There was everything to do at the camp.

Blue closed the door on the toaster, glad to get away from the stifling milk room with its squalid proofs of failure.

But he couldn't sleep that night. The wind in the pine trees sounded like breathy harmonica music. He started to drift off, then heard the papery rush of mice overhead in the loft and the toaster shot into his mind like a chromed comet, then came a plan to finish off the raw, sad loft as a little studio apartment. Then the toaster again. He imagined Gilbert dropping the plates on the floor, excited by the act of fracturing, stealing the toaster. There was a kind of person who had to break things for pleasure. The loft could be made into a bedroom, a living room and kitchenette, cupboards and closets. The walls had to be sheetrocked and painted cream color, a roof skylight set in; there had to be a brass bed with a blue coverlet. Gilbert had taken the toaster because it was shiny, not because he wanted toast, Blue thought, remembering how grandly it sat on the table where the light could play on its curves. He told himself, at last falling into

sleep, that it probably reminded Gilbert of the stolen hubcaps of
his youth.

The next day the rankling thoughts of the toaster receded as
he set panes of glass, scrubbed the floors. He spent hours rubbing the black, dented pots with steel wool, raising the old metal
to a dull gleam like the pewter surface of a twilight pond.

A few days went by, the snow slumped in the sunlight while
Blue repaired steps, painted shutters, nailed new shingles to the
roof. He trimmed and pruned away the lower branches of the
trees around the house.

A faint thread of unease stitched his work. The bright nails
seemed sometimes to sink deep with a single powdery blow as
if the underlying wood was rotten; the dry old shutters were as
light as cardboard; he patched the bright shingles onto wracked
and splintered neighbors that might not last; the heartwood of
the tree branches he sawed was black. But in the end the camp
was transformed. He couldn't get enough of looking at the place.

When only a few days were left before his flight home, the radio droned news of a storm corkscrewing up the coast with gale
winds and heavy snow. The Carolinas were frozen to the heart,
the storm already lashed New Jersey and trains were stalled in
great drifts. A sharp and pleasurable excitement rolled over Blue.
The storm would test the camp, would measure his sufficiency
in danger. He made a list of things he needed to weather it out.
The first word he wrote was "toaster."

He could smell the storm coming, a metallic odor like wet
copper. The natural light was grey and coarse and when he
switched on the electric bulb over the sink the weak incandes-
cent glow drained away like dirty water.

He rushed along the path to the car, anxious to get back before the snow began.

He knocked on the milk room door and waited a long time before Mr. Fitzroy opened it. The old man's eyes were as red as a
St. Bernard's, his mouth slack. He was wearing a long green flan-
nel nightgown.

"I want the toaster," said Blue. His voice was firm, but not hard, full of the quiet strength learned in the Strength Through Will seminars. He tried to look in Mr. Fitzroy's eyes, but they stared away at some ghostly thing in the trees.

"I'm not going to say anything to the sheriff about how Gilbert messed up our camp unless I have to, but I want that toaster," said Blue. He tried to step into the milk room, but Mr. Fitzroy set his hands on each side of the doorframe and blocked him, still staring out and away as if directions for what to do next were printed in the sky. Blue pulled at the old man's arms. They were as corded and hard as alder branches. He heaved and twisted, first at one arm, then the other, until he pried Mr. Fitzroy loose.

"Gilbert," called the old man in the mangled voice of someone having a nightmare. But Gilbert slept like a dead hog under the covers of the bed he and Mr. Fitzroy shared, nor did he move when Blue seized the toaster and carried it to his car. Light glinted on the old man's wet lip.

At the supermarket Blue bought all the things he should not, marshmallows and cocoa mix, cream-filled pastries, almond tarts, frozen lemon pie, bread, butter and a jar of strawberry preserves for the toast.

The snow pecked at the car on the way back, thickened and clogged the windshield wipers. The car slid on the corners and he was trembling when at last he reached the track to the camp. Snow hissed in the spruce needles and rattled against the grocery bags in his arms as he tramped back to the camp.

In the snug kitchen he plugged in the toaster and inserted slices of bread, stoked the fire and pulled his chair up to the stove. The storm slashed at the windows and he made piece after piece of toast, stacking them up on a plate. He set out the almond tarts, mixed the cocoa and put the lemon pie beside the stove to defrost. But his willpower allowed him only two dry pieces of toast while clear drops like tears gathered on the surface of the shriveling meringue and opaque skin sealed the cocoa.

The grey hours deepened in tone as the snow changed, first to enormous pinwheels of matted flakes, then to silvery, slanted lines of sleet. By night, rain streamed down the windows, tangled strings of wind wound the house. He thought he heard a loud drip beat on the floor of the loft as though the roof leaked, but when he went upstairs and shone the flashlight around the empty space he could see nothing but dry dust and orderly shadows. The camp was sound.

He packed his rucksack the next morning, swept the floor and adjusted the dish towel on the bar to hang evenly. He piled the stale, untasted sweets and cakes onto a plate and strode out into the sunlight pouring through a rent in the sky's fabric. The rain had washed away the snow except for the drifts at the foot of the ledge and sodden grey shawls under the trees.

He pitched the pastry away, watched the lemon pie fall and break in smears of cloudy gel where the sun ignited the coarse snow into a white blinding pit. The almond tarts skittered like crabs, the stiff bread pinwheeled.

In the pit, brittle rods of light broke off the curved chrome side of a toaster stamped with a design of wheat sheaves, still half-sunk in the drift. It was their old toaster, looking as hot and glittering as the day it was hurled across the kitchen and he could not understand how he had mistaken another for it.

The Wer-Trout

SAUVAGE and Rivers are neighbors for a year before they meet. Sauvage and his wife live in a trailer a mile beyond the Riverses' house. Rivers has noticed the wife driving the Jeep up from the mailbox at the base of the mountain, her animal-brown hair long and tangled, shooting away from her head like dark, charged wires, her beaked nose, bloodless lips, black eyes like wet stones. The invisible husband, Sauvage, is away at work early and late, the soft purling of his truck's descent half-heard an hour before dawn, the nocturnal return a fiery wink of taillights from the kitchen window before he turns the curve and vanishes into the tunnel of trees above. Rivers often waves at the woman, thinking of country neighbors, of a little mountain gossip, and maybe of something more. She never waves back; her black eyes are locked on distant sights.

It is the same this May morning. Rivers is driving down to his shop, The March Brown. She is driving up from the mailbox. As he lifts his hand, she turns her head away. He makes a certain gesture, an angry bunch of fingers from the days when his father's name was Riverso—Misfortune, Reverse, Wrong Side. He smooths his thick, white hair, looking into the rearview mirror. He is not an old fool yet. Calm, calm, he thinks, and recites an ancient Chinese poem:

> On the southern slopes flocks of crows make their home,
> On the northern slopes people set nets to catch them.
> But when they fly, inaccessible on the winds,
> Of what use then are nets and bird traps?

❦ ❦ ❦

Bitch, he thinks, Mrs. Crow Bitch dressed in black wool and living on the south slope of the mountain, evading the traps of neighbors' pleasantries. Has she seen that gesture? His wife calls her bitch, too. His wife's hands are serious, with tapered fingers as smooth as white jade. She embroiders birds on linen. A museum has published a book of her designs with lists of matching silk colors. *The American Bittern*—celadon, pearl, medium dove, *tête de Nègre,* fawn, faded meadow grass. She calls herself a needlecrafter and poses by the window in a brocade slipper chair. Her spare needles lie on the mahogany sewing table like a school of minnows. In her fingers a metallic shiver trails thread as fine as child's hair, but there is a curious sense of dreary labor in the finished work.

She phones him at the shop later that morning. He leaves a blue dun poised in the vise. Outside the south wind cracks the glossy end branches of the trees like whips.

"That goddamn woman—" He knows who she means. "That crazy, rat-haired bitch, she drove right across the yard, smashed the little apple tree, went through the garden, then back onto the road and up the mountain."

This is the first year of bloom for the Golden Russet. White blossoms are loosely scattered in its crown like a drifting cloud of mayflies. His wife says the top half of the tree now hangs upside down nearly touching the lawn, held to the main trunk only by a strip of bark. She can see the bull's-eye center of its heartwood. There are four great curved furrows in the earth from the Jeep's tires.

"A great little couple," she says, her voice twanging hard as a knotted linen cord. "Her and that husband that's never around. Got your eye on her too, haven't you? Our neighbors. A great place you picked to live, here. A fishing alky who can't make a living and crazy neighbors, that's what *I* end up with." She slams down the receiver. He can hear finality. She has had enough for a long time and says so, often.

At noon she calls again. There is a sound like lightning in the wire. Here it comes, he thinks. She says she is going back to the city, taking her bird designs, her sewing box, her watercolors of wild mushrooms, and the bottles of vitamin pills. He can have the rest. He knows this speech, has heard it before, how he lured her away from her city friends to live on a back road where tongue-tied, hostile natives squat in claptrap trailers. She names his faults and bad habits, then says she is not getting any younger. He has what *he* wants, but she has nothing. Her voice rings plangent with self-pity. He feels angry, but what she says is true. He has his own pleasure in The March Brown, with its custom-tied flies, antique rods, imported English creels and old fishing prints, his books of Chinese poetry. He likes the snugness of the shop in winter with the stove kicking out breakers of heat, the glint of a fallen piece of peacock herl, the stacked boxes of moose mane, wild-turkey wing, hare masks, and grizzly necks. The March Brown, steadily losing the retirement money, silently eating up his golden-age coin, and the sad, subtle poems about autumn mist, fallen leaves, and flowing water putting out his last sparks of ambition. He doesn't know if this is contentment or deadly inertia. Let her go embroider her goddamn birds. One can live cheaper than two.

He comes home at dusk. Her car is gone, and already the house has assumed a different aspect, an angular flatness. The lawn is plowed and scored not with four, but with hundreds of deep grooves. The apple tree is a flattened knot of broken branches. Is this his wife's goodbye, or Sauvage's wife's hello? Will he find, inside his door, Mrs. Bitch, her black skirts bunched and pulled up behind, wagging them at him like the quivering tail display of a lustful female crow? He notices that the sky fits like a dove's breast between the bud-swollen branches of maple. There is no one inside the house, nor a letter of goodbye. The vitamin pills and Dr. Bronner's Breakfast Tonic are gone. The living room seems to have arched its ceiling higher, the chair legs are more graceful, the window glass brilliantly clear, holding the dulling light for long minutes before the dark. Red taillights go up the mountain—Sauvage homeward bound. The familiar fragrance of his wife is still in the room, will be for a long time. Li Bo, he thinks.

> *. . . though the scent remains*
> *In person she'll not come again*
> *A love that is* something, something *falling*
> *Or white dew wet on the* something *moss*

He tries a stiff sob, but it is for Li Bo, not his gone wife. Sauvage's headlights are coming back down the mountain, yellow torches flaring through the hardwoods, first to east, then to west on the switchbacks, then along the straight and into the driveway. He will apologize for the multiple tire trenches in the lawn or perhaps bear a last message from the vanished embroiderer.

Sauvage has a French-Canadian face, long and narrow with skin the color of neutral shoe polish, a nose made for the nasalities of *joual*. There are circles around his eyes like bruises. He is twenty years younger than Rivers. He folds a card in his small fingers and folds again.

"I got trouble up home. Hey, I got to use your phone?" He has on a black-and-red checked wool cap of the type favored by old deer hunters, brown cotton twill work pants, and felt-lined pac-boots. There is a draggled Dark Cahill in his hat. "I got to use your phone," he says again. "I come home, my wife's eating a mouse. She don't talk, just eating it there with the skin on—" He gags, recovers.

Rivers thinks of that pale mouth reddened. A piece of wet gravel falls from the edge of Sauvage's boot onto the floor with an infinitesimal tick.

"She put the phone in the sink, it's full of hot water. I got to call her doctor. She has these troubles." There is an upward rock to the rhythm of his sentences.

Rivers points to his wall phone and goes into the living room out of courtesy, closing the door behind him. He hears a murmur, coughing, then the outside kitchen door closing. The red tail-lights go steadily back up the mountain.

Later the ambulance rushes up, a bonfire flying through the trees. Rivers leans against the cold window, his breath clouding the glass and obscuring the reflection of his aging face. It has begun to rain, spring rain, good for young apple trees, good for young trout. The ambulance descends, its headlights shining on the curved lakes that fill the wheel ruts in his ruined lawn. Sauvage trails behind in his truck, solitary mourner in a cortege.

Rivers has a sense of narrow escape from disaster, like the victim of an earthquake who sees the houses on each side in dust-plumed rubble while his own is untouched. He feels that some powerful divine force has summoned away the two women who lived on the south side of the mountain. Well, they had to take their turns at misery; he has had his, he thinks, years before, the drinker stuttering into the glass caverns of bottles, so wounded by the circumstances of his wretched life that it seemed the knots of his heart could never be unpicked, even with an awl. He has found a way to cure himself of all suffering and worry by memorizing ancient Chinese poems and casting artificial flies in moving water. He is solaced by the faint parallels between his own perception of events and those of the stringy-bearded scholars of the Tang, enjoying, as he does, a sad peace at the sight of feathered ephemera balanced on the dark-flowing river.

In bed he reads the paper. A woman has found god through a car accident, saying, "What happened to me brought out my religion like crazy." Below this is a one-line filler: "Some say to dream of doves means happiness." Rivers has heard his wife say this differently—"Bird dreams mean sunbeams." But in fact how many people do dream of doves? Ornithologists? Hawkish politicians who wake in hot sweats of resentment rather than happiness? "Dream of trout," says Rivers in his bed.

He dreams of a crow. A malignant crow with a red eye like a rock bass. Human fat glistens on its beak, as cruelly curved as secateurs. A glint of light burns on the steely edge and becomes a flashing needle, the crow itself an embroidered bird worked by the erratic electric impulses of his sleeping brain. He wakes, his heart flailing like a netted trout. The window is a grey rectangle in the blackness of the wall. He hears an engine laboring up the mountain. Sauvage going back to his trailer.

It is still raining in the morning when he goes to The March Brown. The black locust trees lean against the stained sky, the water on the road hisses. There are no customers all morning.

In the afternoon he is reading how Yuan Mei's cook falls ill with hallucinations and thinks sunlight is snow, when Sauvage comes in. He is bigger than he was in the kitchen. He says he has stopped by to thank Rivers for the use of his phone last night. He looks around the shop. The rain still beats against the window, but inside it is warm, scented with fine oils and dry feathers, with burning beech, seasoned bamboo, and the thin, intoxicating odor of head cement. Certain emanations come from the shelf of Chinese poets—the returning boat, moon water, and river weeds. Sauvage seems calm, as calm as Rivers. He looks beyond the streaming window, deciding some private matter.

"You know the Yellow Bogs?" Sauvage asks, leaning on the counter and cocking his right leg comfortably. Neither wants to talk about vanished needlecrafters or mad rodent appetites. "Yellow Bogs is up in the north." There are stoic folds at the corners of his mouth. He knows of the place because of his grandfather's stories. The old man worked up in the north-country swamps in the early twenties, cutting timber and pulp. Sauvage has never been there himself, but he knows the fables of the country and can salt his sentences with Quebecois expletives.

The Logger Brook, the Yellow Branch, and the Black Branch come thrashing down the steep mountains through a tangle of deadfalls and slash, in company with fifty nameless streams and brooks. All this water flattens out in the Bogs in random sloughs and ponds. Black fountains well up like the fuming outlets of an underground river flowing in secret torrents through cavities under the mountains. Sauvage murmurs, drawing invisible lines across the counter with his yellow fingers. Rivers feels the floor of The March Brown shift under his feet like flooding sand.

Yes, says Sauvage, that Yellow Bogs is bad country. Bear hunters lose their dogs in there. Once a team of horses went down in a bottomless pool, dragging the driver with them below the stinking black mud. It is cold in the Bogs, shrouded in thick mists and rain, and August snow stings the swamp maples. The drops of moisture on the tips of the spruce branches never dry before rain falls again. Rivers can hear the northern rain stored in the empty woods, hear it falling on the humped boulders at the water's edge.

Sauvage leans closer, his finger taps, and he says that in the cold, rain-stippled rivers, in the deep sinkholes of Yellow Bogs, there are native brook trout. Old trout. Giants of the water. Some of them, says Sauvage, go over eight pounds. In his inner eye Rivers sees the Yellow Bogs shaped like a huge black bottle, and himself, smaller than a mote of dust, drawn into the neck by an invisible current of desire.

Sauvage and Rivers jounce on the front seat of the truck. The logging road marked on the topographical map has fallen back to wilderness in the decades since the last survey. Twice they prize the truck out of mudholes with a cut poplar for a lever, Sauvage lunging, Rivers rocking the wallowing vehicle as the wheels spin out gouts of cold mud. Thick snow still lies in the northern hollows. The road vanishes before they reach the Bogs.

"Shank's mare!" cries Rivers in a new, high-pitched voice. It is late afternoon, the air chilly and raw after the snug truck cab. Sauvage takes up the small canoe like a cross.

Rivers walks in front with a heavy pack, an adversary that tries to pull him to the ground. Sauvage's right to go first is stronger because of his grandfather's presence sixty years earlier on this same trail, but Rivers burns with hotter lust to penetrate the Bogs. He has brought his old Garrison bamboo rod, his favorite when he was a young man, a rod with memories. Sauvage's rod is a cheap, discount-store bargain.

After half a mile they rest. Sauvage smokes a cigarette. Rivers sucks the smell of leaf mold and wet ferns into his nose. There is a burning spot between his shoulder blades coming from the whiskey bottles carefully wrapped and buried in the depths of the pack. They send out a feeling like a hot-water bottle and he feels safe in their company, although he has not had a drink for six years and has taught himself to think of alcohol as a corrosive lye that will burn out his liver and lights. The embroiderer made him take an oath never to drink again. He remembers the fluttering candle, himself naked on his knees on the pine floor, his right hand held high, his fervent swearing never, never to take another drink of alcohol, not sherry, not rum, not beer, and certainly never whiskey, while the woman in the ice-blue satin nightgown embroidered all around the hem with stooping falcons smiled down on him with wet and gleaming teeth.

The light seeps from the sky as they go along the faint trail. Swamp chill comes up from the ground and mosquitoes whine. A pale strip of water glimmers through the trees, and Rivers has a sense of pleasant loneliness, of being at the edge of a cliff. It is Yellow Bogs. The light bleeds away and a dark angle of shadow spreads over the water. The waterweeds go a deep, sinking black.

Rivers struggles to put up the tent. In the west a heavy roll of clouds holds a deep bronze patina. A mosquito hawk rows through the lake of sky like a feathered boat, his wings trailing a stuttering sound. The yellow flames of Sauvage's fire leap, and Rivers frames words with his lips: "How about a drink?" He does not say them. It is all for himself, and he can still wait a little longer.

Sauvage cries, "Tomorrow, big trout watch out! I hope I brought a frying pan big enough to hold one of them big ones. Hey, Rivers, how you like this place?"

"Feels like home," says Rivers.

"Gives me the creeps in the dark," answers Sauvage. A few drops of rain fall, each a spit in the fire. The silence has a heavy weight. Rivers thinks a little of the Five-bottle Scholar, Wang Chi, who died from overindulgence in wine. There are worse ways.

This habit of his of sinking backward into the past sets him outside the events of the present. Everything has happened before: the deaths of children, the house burning in the night, the barred shadows of poplars lying across the road in late autumn, sharp-toothed illness biting into soft bones, loneliness, the village scourged by bearded invaders, the people cruelly tortured, a drunken reveler singing a half-forgotten verse in the dusk, the scent of bruised grass, the emptied cup, the slow wingbeat of a dying crow. He recognizes himself as a struggling spentwing floating briefly on time's river. Before he falls asleep in the faintly musty tent, he touches some of his shining bottles. The rain comes across the Bogs and onto the tent like an iron threshing machine in a prairie wheat field.

His watch says 5:20. Fine cold points of mist touch his face, then dissolve in the heat from his body. He crawls out into the dim morning. Larch branches like severed arms writhe and float in the fog. Yellow Bogs is hidden behind opaque layers of mist, and the drenched earth runs in streams and rivulets.

There is Sauvage, kneeling in front of a neat pyramid of shaved dead spruce branches, their dry hearts exposed, curls of birch bark bunched underneath. In a second the flames catch. A wavering globe of orange light hangs in the mist around him, his long face still creased with the lines of sleep. Rivers is contrary this morning; he does not want fire and breakfast, he wants to find the secret pools in Yellow Bogs where the giant trout lie waiting, their fins gently strumming the water.

But Sauvage wants to stay on the margin, fishing the edge of the Bogs. "How about keep this camp until the fog burns off?" he says. "I seen this thick stuff hang in most of the day. Look at it, you don't see thirty feet."

"This is only the edge. We get any trout in here, they'll be fleas," mutters Rivers. The *lunkers*—he says—will be deep in the coiled entrail of the Bogs, maybe a two-day journey in. "We got to make some time," he says. "No point in coming two hundred miles up here to catch midget trout."

They paddle in silence, the wet tent bunched between them. The water narrows, broadens, narrows again. Sauvage looks left and right, over each shoulder. Spruce, larch and cedar, monotonously similar, loom from unsuspected shores, then fall away.

"Islands," says Sauvage. Then, mournfully, "Jesus, in here less than a day and I bet we're lost."

"Not lost," lies Rivers. "I got the direction all lined out. Been following the main current. Got my compass." He has the reckless feeling that nothing matters except going forward. A willow leaf curves away from them and they can hear the muffled rushing of stream water into the Bogs away to their right. They drag the canoe over barriers of wedged and woven sticks and branches in stout beaver dams. Channels twist and curve, dozens of tiny streams and rivulets tinkle and splash into the grass-choked marshy perimeter of the Bogs. The water is brown and deep. Once Rivers sees a submerged log move, a trick of the cloudy water or the ponderous drift of a big fish. Trout are here. He can smell them. Nymphs, he thinks, maybe where the streams run in, maybe go up some of the bigger brooks a little way. Wet flies, black gnats, spentwings, everything drowning, wet, underwater, and lost in tail-churned mud or shroudlike fog. But there is enmity in Sauvage's paddling, and Rivers thinks it is too early for that. Rivers guides them to a small sandbar under the cracked arm of a cedar.

There is a snug sense of shelter under the trees. Rivers sets up the tent, a silent apology to Sauvage for pushing ahead in bad weather. "We can stay here a few days if the fishing's good, wait for the weather to break," he says. "We're in pretty deep now, anyway."

Sauvage quickly makes a solid fireplace with a double ring of stones. "Think we're on an island?"

"Don't know. Dumb to go any farther in this fog. It's got to lift sometime, and while we wait we can try the water."

Sauvage looks into his cheap plastic fly case while Rivers looks over the characterless spread of water, flattened and smoothed by the heavy mist like a bolt of satin by a warm iron. Then they hear it. Somewhere out on the flat water behind the cape of muffling fog a ponderous weight plunges down, a vast splash like a granite monument falling into the Bogs.

"What the hell was that?" says Sauvage.

"One of the big ones." It is only what Rivers has expected.

"No, no," says Sauvage, "they don't come *that* big. Had to be a beaver. A big buck beaver telling us to get the hell out of his territory. Slap his tail, you know?" Then another crashing plunge, nearer in the mist. Not the sharp crack of a flat beaver tail on the smooth water, but the rushing collapse of a wall of water into a monstrous cavity. Rivers can easily imagine a tremendous trout the size of a gun case, but the splash is followed by a thick, coughing cry that dies away in the reeds.

"Sweet Jesus," says Sauvage.

"What the hell, let's fish," says Rivers.

"Maybe stick together, though," says Sauvage.

In a flash of intuition Rivers knows Sauvage is afraid of what he cannot see, maybe haunted by the mysterious behavior of his wife, or by the French-Canadian grandfather stories of loup-garou, of windigo, evil forests, and swamp demons, of all the dark riddles of superstition.

He looks at the water. Strange water, not the dead onyx mirror of a bog pond, but the swollen overflow of a dammed river. The main current pulses faintly eastward. He has felt it against his paddle all morning. Before him lies a deep, eddying pool out of the current's main thrust. He thinks he sees moving shadows near the bottom. Onshore the blackflies are bad. Rivers takes a tiny number twenty-two black midge nymph from his case irresolutely; the grey mist and bad light—maybe something flashier. But he ties it on anyway. Sauvage, seventy feet above him, gives a cry and Rivers turn to see his arm curved in a familiar arch, the rod tip down and an orange-bellied brookie the size of a young bass boring into the water. Sauvage is deft but not delicate. He tends to haul in the trout, cutting short the sweet struggle.

"Nice one!" he congratulates himself, giving Rivers a triumphant smirk. Rivers sees that Sauvage is a competitor; an aggressive, posturing contest winner, not someone who can understand self-made solitude.

Rivers turns away and thinks himself deep for the trout, casts the tiny weighted midge and watches the line, waiting for the halt or the trembling leap forward. Nothing. He starts it back to him in tiny jerks, lets it rest, again the miniature, tender twitch and a trout takes it just under the surface, smashing the water, tail walking, rearing up like a sea serpent, and writhing its muscular body in the fluid river like a corkscrew. Then it is over. The fish comes down on the fine tippet and breaks it, running for the bottom with Rivers's little black nymph. Sauvage, who has been watching, whinnies.

"You smart-ass bastard," says Rivers to the spreading ring on the water, "I'm going to get you."

At two o'clock Rivers starts the first bottle. He sits on a stump, taking good swallows from it and watching Sauvage cook his trout. He has skewered the thick, limp bodies on peeled willow sticks and set them over a circle of coals. The delicate membrane of ash is disturbed by smoking drops that fall from the fish. The trout twist in a semicircle as though they are trying to bite their own flanks, like dogs after fleas. Sauvage peels the cooked flesh from the laddered backbones in steaming orange chucks. Rivers refuses to eat.

"I didn't catch any yet. I'll wait."

"That's funny, you didn't catch *anything?* I thought you was

the Great Fisherman. Me, I caught what, five, six? Big ones, too.
By god, they taste good. What you using?"

"Dry flies," lies Rivers.

"Look, you oughta try wets or try some of them nymphs. Here,
sometimes the real little ones are good. I used this one to get
these here." Patronizingly he stretches out his hand to Rivers.

"Where'd you get this?" says Rivers, sure that he recognizes
the too-big head and the off-kilter wings of the number twenty-
two black midge nymph he lost a few hours earlier.

"Had it a long time," answers Sauvage, eating a trout as he
would a slice of watermelon.

In an hour Rivers is halfway down the bottle and sets off
through the woods looking for private water. His steps seem
cushioned on thick, matted grass, but there is only spruce duff
and an occasional etiolated fern clump underfoot. It is the
whiskey that makes the ground so yielding. The trees seem to
shift away from him slyly on both sides, but he marches in a
straight line through the swampy hummocks and wet, slapping
branches until he finds the water again, hung with opaque shawls
of wooly grey, a solitary place, pungent with decay, and far away
from Sauvage. The bottle is his companion.

His waders and hat are in the tent. He takes his clothes off except for his boots and walks into the water to escape the knotted
alders, pulling the Yellow Bogs around him like a cold sheet. His
shirt is wound about his head against the blackflies. For the next
hours he makes a superb series of casts, running through everything in his repertoire and his monogrammed leather fly case, for
the water is changeable, shaping itself before his eyes, first into
glassy pools, then frothy falls, rapid snaking currents, yellow ribbons of crumpled silk over sandbars, deep onyx mines of still
water bent under sunless vaults of alder, milky absinthe cloud
runs of chalk stream, and the stump-pocked moon face of a
beaver pond. The trout torment him with their wavering outlines.
He sees the elliptical underwater silver of trout rooting in the
gravel, big browns lying like corpses on their own shadows,

nymph-feeding rainbows bulging the water into hilly landscapes, fly takers sucking holes in the fragile tissue of the surface film, leaping brookies trying for flying morsels on the wing like cats after sparrows. He catches nothing, a white-haired, shivering fool with a tired arm and an empty whiskey bottle. He dresses again and wanders back through light evening rain to the wet tent and Sauvage.

Sauvage has an enormous fire burning and sits within the circle of light peering out at the crawling shadows under the black spruce. "Jesus, where the hell you been! I been waiting here for a couple of hours. I thought you mighta fell in and drowned." Sauvage fussily unwraps a silver cigar of aluminum foil, disclosing the baked bodies of two large brook trout.

One of them, a good fifteen inches long, wounds Rivers's heart that someone other than he should have caught it. He goes into the tent and gets the second bottle. "I don't want any fish. You eat them," he says.

Sauvage pouts like a spurned bride while the rain falls on the hot trout, diluting the juices. Sauvage begins to eat mournfully, with every mouthful looking up at Rivers on the stump, the rain dripping off the underside of his upraised bottle.

"There's somebody else here in the Bogs," Sauvage says suddenly. "I seen him."

"Yeah? Who is it, the fish cop?"

"No. I don't think so. He looks like he's crazy, a crazy fisherman. He's fishing over there across the channel. First I see only this shape, this human shape, casting and casting. Then the fog lifts a little and I can see the guy pretty good. He's buck naked, standing there in that cold water up to his knees, no waders, no vest, and over his head he's got some kind of cloth so I don't see his face. Casts—roll casts, S-casts, bow-and-arrow, double-hauls—everything, just like at an exhibition. So I yell at him, 'Any luck?' but he don't answer. Then the mist comes down heavy again, and the way it comes in, see, it makes it look like the guy starts walking out into the deep water, looks like he goes right down under the water."

"Sauvage, we got real trouble now," says Rivers from behind his bottle. "What you saw was the Wer-Trout, the Wer-Trout of Yellow Bogs."

"Hey, come on, Rivers, don't make jokes about that kind of stuff."

"No joke, Sauvage, that's what you saw. The body of a man, the head of a trout. That's why he covered up his face, so you couldn't see those big, flat eyes and no chin and ugly teeth. Don't worry, though, he only goes for you if you kill his women. You didn't catch any girl trouts, did you?"

Sauvage's grease-dappled chin shines at Rivers in the firelight. "I think you're drunk, Rivers," he says.

Rivers laughs stagily. He feels his words falling as precise as snowflakes, as luminous as sunlight. "Yeah? Remember that big splash we heard? That you said was a beaver? That was the Wer-Trout. Thank god *I* didn't catch any of his pals. And what was that you said to him? 'Any luck?'! Christ, he'll really be after you now. Also, Sauvage, that's how come our wives are gone. In the daytime when we weren't there the Wer-Trout came around, showed his face in the window, and scared them away. That's why the little ladies always go."

"Knock it off, Rivers. We come out here to do some fishing, get away from our troubles, and you go off half the day, get drunk, start this kind of talk. I think we head back in the morning."

"Caw, caw, caw," says Rivers, showing his teeth and winking both eyes. Sauvage, insulted, crawls into the tent. Rivers stays up, blowing across the neck of his bottle, making a sound like a coyote in a cider barrel. After a while he notices a tiny scurrying shape at the morsels of fish Sauvage has let drop on the ground. He stalks the mouse with his bottle for a weapon, his thumb thrust into the neck against spillage, and mashes it dead with temporary dexterity. He places it in the center of Sauvage's frying pan, where it sticks in the congealing grease, then goes back to his stump.

He comes to, lying in the pricking rain near the stump, his body convulsed with shivers, his teeth clacking. He feels wizened and cold to the heart. The fire is a stinking black circle of muddy ash as he crawls over it toward the tent, hoping he won't throw up in the sleeping bag. It hurts to breathe, to move, to live. Just beyond the stump his knee comes down on something like a slender twig. The sound is only a small, dry crack, but Rivers knows at once what it is. He has been dreading that inevitable sound for more than twenty years, and it is as sharp as an embroidery needle thrust into his eardrum. He has broken his Garrison bamboo. He picks it up in the dark, the upper half dangling uselessly like his snapped apple tree. He thinks he can feel its spirit dribbling out of the crushed hexagonal heart like a string of hardening wax. His apple tree is dead, his lawn ruined, his wife gone, his Garrison broken, and he has caught no fish nor will catch any now. Yet he tells himself these transitory ills are like duckweed on the water. There is no mouse on his plate.

Inside the tent he lights a candle and unwraps the last bottle from his wife's blue satin nightgown. In the shining curve of glass he sees his reflection: the chinless throat, the pale snout, the vacant rusted eyes of the Wer-Trout.

Electric Arrows

1

"YOU tell me," says Reba, wrapped up in her blue sweater with the metal buttons. She's wearing the grey sweatpants again. Her head is tipped back steeply on the long neck column as she looks up at me, her narrow rouged mouth like a red wire. "Tell me why anybody in his right mind would sit in The Chicken swilling beer, watching fat men wrestle until midnight, why?"

I think, so they don't have to sit around in the kitchen and look at moldy pictures.

Aunt pulls one out as thick as a box lid. I see milkweed blowing, the house set square on a knob of lawn, each nailhead hard, the shadows of the clapboards like black rules.

There is a colorless, coiled hair on Reba's sweater sleeve.

"I couldn't believe it, open the door of that place and there you are," she says.

Aunt's finger traces along the side of the picture, over the steep maples, over a woman with two children standing in the white road. Aunt smells of lemon lotion and clothes worn two days to save on laundry detergent. The faces in the photograph are round plates above dark shoulders, smiles like fern fronds. The woman holds a blurred baby, she holds him forever. The other child is unsmiling, short and stocky, a slap of black hair across his forehead. He died of cholera a few weeks after they took the photograph.

Aunt points to the baby and says, "That's your father." He is unfocused, leached by the far sunlight. She clasps her thick, hard old palms together.

"I'm grateful I was there, Reba, when you come along needing your flat tire changed," I say.

"That part was good," she murmurs, as if giving me something I'd long coveted.

We are at the kitchen table inside the house of the photograph, waiting for the pie to cool. The camera belonged to Leonard Prittle, the hired man, who lived in this house once. We don't have a hired man now, we don't have a farm, we live in the house ourselves. Reba encourages Aunt with the photographs. And the Moon-Azures, hey, the damn Moon-Azures think the past belongs to them.

"Want me to whip the cream to go on the pie?" I ask Reba.

I do go down to The Chicken sometimes.

The maples in the photograph are all gone, cut when they widened the road. There is Aunt at the wheel of a Reo truck with her hair bobbed. The knuckles are smooth in the pliant hand. They widened the road, but they didn't straighten it.

Aunt takes another picture and another, she can't stop. She lifts them, the heavy-knuckled fingers precise and careful, her narrow Clew head bent and the pale Clew eyes roving over the images of black suits and ruched sleeves, dead children, horses with braided manes, a storm cloud over the barn. She says, "Leonard Prittle could of been something if he'd of had a chance."

Reba cuts the pie into seeping crimson triangles. Back when she worked she gave kitchen parties to show farm women how to get the most of their freezers and mixers. Now it's all microwaves and the farm women live in apartments in Concord.

I pretend to look at the picture. The weathervanes point at an east wind. There are picket fences, elm trees, a rooster in the weeds. Hey, I've seen that rooster picture a hundred times.

Time has scraped away the picket fences, and you should hear the snowplow throw its dirty spoutings against the clapboards; it sounds like the plow is coming through the kitchen. The leftover

Pugleys, Clews and the Cuckhorns live in these worn-out houses. Reba was a Cuckhorn.

"Properties break apart," says Aunt, sighing and nipping off the pie point with her fork. We know how quarreling sons sell sections of the place to Boston schoolteachers, those believers that country life makes you good. When they find it does not, they spitefully sell the land again, to Venezuelan millionaires, Raytheon engineers, cocaine dealers and cold-handed developers.

Reba mumbles, "The more you expect from something, the more you turn on it when it disappoints you."

I suppose she means me.

Aunt and I still own a few acres of the place—the hired man's house, where we live, and the barn. *Atlantic Ocean Farm* is painted on the barn door because my father, standing on the height of land as a young man full of hopeful imagination, thought he saw a shining furrow of sea far to the east between a crack in the mountains.

Reba puts plastic wrap over the uneaten pie, turns up the television sound. I go walk in the driveway before the light's gone. Through the barn window I can see empty cardboard appliance boxes stacked inside, soft and shapeless from years of damp.

You can see how nothing has changed in the barn. A knotted length of baling twine, furry with dust, still stretches from the top of the ladder to a beam. The kite's wooden skeleton, a fragile cross, is still up there.

I could take it down.

There is the thick snoring of a car turning in the driveway. It's not dark enough for the headlights, just the fog lights, set wide apart, yellow. The Moon-Azures. They don't see me by the barn. Mrs. Moon-Azure opens the car door and sticks out her legs as straight as celery stalks.

I go back in the house, let the cat in. Moon-Azure says, "Nice evening, Mason." His eyeglasses reflect like the fog lights. "Thought I'd see if you could give me a hand tomorrow. The old willow went down, and it looks like we need a tug with the tractor."

More like half a day's work.

When I look out the window I can see Yogetsky's trailer with the crossed snowshoes mounted over the door, the black mesh satellite dish in front of the picture window. Yogetsky is an old bachelor. His cranky, shining kitchen is full of saved tin cans, folded plastic bags, magazines piled in four-color pyramids. He sets bread dough to rise on top of the television set.

Across the road from his trailer there's the Beaubiens' place. The oldest son's log truck is parked in the driveway, bigger than the house. A black truck with the word *Scorpion* in curly script. The Beaubiens are invisible, maybe behind the truck, maybe inside the house, eating baked beans out of a can, sharing the fork. They eat quick, afraid of losing time that could be put into work. King Olaf sardines, jelly roll showing the crimson spiral inside the plastic wrap, Habitant pea soup.

Yogetsky moved up from Massachusetts about ten years ago and got two jobs, one to live on, the other to pay his property taxes, he says. His thick nose sticks out of his face like a cork. He says, "This trailer, this land," pointing at the shaved jowl of lawn, "is a investment. Way people are coming in, it'll be worth plenty, year or two."

He owns two acres of Pugley's old cow pasture.

Yogetsky is a reader. He takes *USA Today* and magazines of the type with stories in them about dentists who become fur trappers. His garden is fenced in with sheep wire. The tops of tin cans hang on the fence and stutter in the wind. There's his flag-pole.

2

We raised apples. Baldwins, Tolman Sweets, Duchess, Snow Apple, Russet and Sheep's Nose. The big growers were pushing the McIntosh and the Delicious. I was nervy and sick, but I had to help my father string barbwire around the orchard and down through the woods. A quick, sloppy job. The deer would come in late June, the young deer, and eat the new tender leaves, still crumpled and folded on the Baldwin seedlings. Nobody knew what was wrong with me. Nervy, Aunt said. Growing too fast. The Baldwins, torn and stripped, grew crooked.

The McIntosh apple ruined us. My father ruined us.

He said, "Children, it's a hard way to go to make money on sugar, but there's a good dollar in the Baldwin apple." And sold the maples for timber. And bought five hundred Baldwin seedlings. Your Baldwin apple is a dull, cloudy maroon color. It's got somewhat of a tender rootstock.

People wanted a shiny, red apple. Our fruit went to the juice mills. Now it's the other way around. All those old kinds we couldn't give away. Black Twig. Pinkham Pie. They pay plenty for them now.

Once your sugar bush is gone, it's gone for fifty years or forever.

My father sold pieces of the woodlot. Then pieces of pasture. Pieces of this, pieces of that. None of the Baldwins made it through a hard winter just before the war.

Aunt bites off the end of a raveling thread instead of using scissors.

Dad could make a nice stone wall, but he'd be off on something else before it got to any length. He preferred barbwire, get it over with. Still, he had a feel for stonework, for the chisel, without the dogged concentration you need for that work. He was silly. His excited ways, his easy enthusiasm made Aunt say he was a fool. I never heard anybody laugh like he did, a seesawing, gasping laugh like he was drowning for air. It was the brother that died young that had all the sense, says Aunt.

He let the farm drip through his fingers like water until only an anxious dampness was left in our palms. And his friend Diamond used to pick up first me, then Bootie, my sister, sliding his old dirty paws up between our legs, putting his tobacco-stained mouth at our narrow necks.

"He don't mean nothin' by it," Dad said, "quit your cryin'."

Dad told us, "The farmer's up against it."

You know where the golf course is, the Meadowlark condominiums, them sloping meadows along the river? He sold that land for twenty an acre. Giving it away, even then. I told this to Yogetsky and he moaned, hit his forehead with the heel of his hand, said, "Jesus Christ."

We were up against it. There wasn't the money to find out what was wrong with me, hey, just all kinds of homemade junk. Bootie and I took boiled carrots to school in our lunch pails; the cow's hooves made a thick sucking noise when we drove her across the marshy place and that sound made me feel I didn't have a chance. You get used to it.

The grand name for the farm, the hundreds of no-good trees in the orchard, the heavy, tearing rolls of barbwire strung through the woods were all for nothing.

3

What can I tell you about the Moon-Azures?

They own the original old Clew homestead with its crooked doorframes and worn stairs, Dr. and Mrs. Moon-Azure from Basiltower, Maryland. I was born in that house.

The Moon-Azures come up from Maryland every June and go back in August. They scrape nine layers of paint off the paneling in the parlor, point out to us the things they do to better the place. They clear out the dump, get a backhoe in to cut a wide driveway. They get somebody to sand the floors. They buy a horse. Dr. Moon-Azure's hands get roughed up when he works on the stone wall. He holds them out and says admiringly, "Look at those hands." A faint smell comes from his clothes, the familiar brown odor of the old house. His wall buckles with the first frost heaves.

The Moon-Azures have weekend guests. We see the cars go by, out-of-state license plates on Mercedes and Saabs. When the wind is right we can hear their toneless voices knocking together like sticks of wood, *tot, tot-tot, tot.* The horse gets out and is killed on the road.

Nobody knows what kind of doctor he is. They go to him when some woman from Massachusetts backs over the edge of the gravel pit. Somebody drives to Moon-Azure's and asks him to come, but he won't. "I don't practice," he says. "Call the ambulance." He offers them the use of his phone.

They walk a good deal. You drive somewhere and here come the Moon-Azures, stumbling through the fireweed, their hands full of wilted branches.

Tolman at the garage says Moon-Azure's a semiretired psychiatrist, but Aunt thinks he's a heart surgeon who lost his nerve in the middle of an operation. He's got good teeth.

Moon-Azure says, "I'll never get used to the way you people let these fine old places run down." He's found the pile of broken slates that came off the old roof. It's been a tin roof since around 1925.

With Mrs. Moon-Azure it's information. What direction is west, when to pick blackberries, oh, kerosene lamps burn kerosene oil? She thought, gasoline. Like to see her try it. In the winter when they're in Florida, the porcupines get into the house, leave calling cards on the floor. "Look," she says, "bunny rabbits." She writes it all down. "My book on country living," she laughs.

She says "maple surple" for a joke.

"How's the hay coming along?" says Moon-Azure.

Once they come on a Saturday morning, smiling, ask Reba to clean house for them, but she says, "No." A teacup rings hard on the saucer.

They ask Marie Beaubien. They pay her more for wiping their tables and making their beds than any man gets running a chain saw.

"How's the hay coming, Lucien?" says Moon-Azure.

"Good," says Beaubien.

We could of used the money.

Marie Beaubien tells us, "White telephones, one in every

room, and a bathroom all pale blue tiles painted with orchids. They got copper pans cost a hundred dollars for each one and more of them than you can count. Antique baskets hanging all over the walls, carpets everywhere."

It's not my taste.

My taste is simpler.

I like to see bare floor boards.

From the first the Moon-Azures are crazy for old deeds and maps of the farm, they trace Clew genealogy as though they bought our ancestors with the land. They like to think the Clews were farmers. He says, "Mason, looks like a good year for hay."

How the hell would I know?

They go down to the town clerk's office and dig up information on the ear notch patterns Clews used 150 years ago to mark their sheep, try to find out if the early Clews did anything. One time they ask us to write down the kinds of apples. The orchards, black rows of heart-rotted trees, belong to them.

But all of their fascination is with the ancestor Clews; living Clews exist, like the Beaubiens, to be used. Dead Clews belong to the property and the property belongs to the Moon-Azures.

The Moon-Azures hire Lucien to clear out the brush and set up fallen stones. When I take Reba and Aunt for a ride up the road sometimes on the weekends you can see the Moon-Azures and their guests walking away from the cemetery, heads a little down as if they are thinking, not *sic transit gloria mundi,* but *this is mine.*

They post all of the land with big white signs stapled on plywood squares and nailed to posts every hundred feet. They set fence everywhere, along the road, up the drive, around the house, through the woods, all split-rail fence. Not an inch of barbwire. But up in the woods the line of trees shows scars like twisted mouths from the wire we strung to keep the deer out of the orchards.

The Moon-Azures are after us, after the Beaubiens, even after Yogetsky for help with things, getting their car going, clearing out the clogged spring, finding their red-haired dog. They need to know how things happened, what things happened. Every year they go back to the city at the end of the summer. Then that changes.

Mrs. Beaubien polishes her spoon with the paper napkin and sifts sugar into her coffee. "The doctor is retired," she says. "They're goin' to stay up here until Christmas, then go off somewhere hot, then come back up here after mud season. Same thing every year from now on."

Aunt says, "Must be nice to have the jingle in your pockets to just run up and down between the nice weather."

"I never known one of them people to stick it out very long," says Mrs. Beaubien. "Wait till they have to scrape the ice off their own windshield. Lucien don't go up there for that, you bet."

I think, bet he will.

The Moon-Azures keep on walking. What else do they have to do after the first black frosts? In the shortening days their friends don't come to visit, and they have only each other to hear their startled exclamations that fallen leaves have a bitter odor, that the hardening earth throws up rods of cloudy ice. They come at us with their clumsy conversation, wasting our time. Beaubien and his son bring them wood and stack it, the autumn shrivels into November.

A week before Thanksgiving here comes Mrs. Moon-Azure again, walking down the field. She knocks on the window, peers in at Aunt. Cockleburs hang on her ankles. Her clothes are the color of oatmeal. Her eyes are grey. The refrigerator switches on as she starts to speak, and she has to repeat herself in a louder voice. "I said, I hear you have some remarkable photographs!"

"Well, they're interesting to us," says Aunt. She has flour on her hands, and dusts it off, slapping her palms against her thighs. She shows some of the pictures, standing them up on edge saying, "Mr. Galloon Heyscape doing the Irish clog, Denman Thompson's oxen, the radio of the two sweethearts, Kiley Druge and his crazy daughter."

"These are important photographs," says Mrs. Moon-Azure in the same way she said, "You ran over my horse," to Clyde Cuckhorn. We see how much she wants them.

Hey, too bad.

"I wonder they don't come right out and ask if we'll sell them," says Aunt after she's gone. "She'd give anything to get her mitts on these pictures. No, these are Clew family photographs, taken by a very gifted hired man, and here they stay."

Leonard Prittle, our hired man, took his pictures from under a large black cloak cast off by my great-grandmother, says Aunt.

How does she know.

What Aunt is afraid of is that the Moon-Azures will pass the pictures around among their weekend guests, that they will find their way into books and newspapers, and we will someday see our grandfather's corpse in his homemade coffin resting on two sawhorses, flattened out on the pages of some magazine and labeled with a cruel caption.

4

Maybe Dad never imagined himself doing anything but selling off the land and dreaming useless apple thoughts, but in the worst of it he got a job. And this was a time when there wasn't any jobs, and he wasn't looking for one. It wasn't even stonework.

Dad's friend, Diamond Ward, was one of those hard grey men who ate deer meat in every season and could fix whatever was broken again and again until nothing was left of the original machine but its function. Diamond was in the Grange, knew what was going on, and he was one of the first in the county to get a job through the Rural Electrification Act. He got my father in with him. The Ironworks County Electric Power Cooperative. Replaced now by Northern Nuclear. We got the alarm in the kitchen that's supposed to go off if there's an accident down there, everybody evacuate in a hurry.

Where to?

The two of them drove around all day in a dark green truck with a painted circle on the side enclosing the letters ICEPC and three bolts of electricity. Everybody called it "The Icepick." Diamond chewed tobacco, and the door on his side was stained brown. Bootie would get in the closet when she heard Diamond coming up the drive.

The kite's paper is gone, burned up in the seasons of August heat under the cracking barn roof.

There was something in my father that had to blow up whatever he did. He got a certain amount of pleasure seeing himself as The Lone Apple-Grower up against a gang of McIntosh men. Now came a chance to be The One Bringing Light to the Farm. He could fool and laugh with people as much as he wanted.

He'd say, "A five-dollar deposit, the price of a pair of shoes, and we'll put the 'lectricity in. You'll hear the radio, hear Amos and Andy." He'd imitate Amos, laugh. "Get rid of them sad irons, use them for doorstops. Lights? Get twict the work done because you'll be able to see the both ends of the cow. *Hawhaw.*"

He got up a mock funeral at the Grange, spent weeks laughing and talking it up. The men carried a coffin around the hall, then took it out and buried it. It was full of oil lamps and blackened chimneys.

Hey, I'm telling you, this is within our lifetime.

Television wasn't invented until 1938.

He'd list the things electricity was going to do away with. No more stinking privies. No more strained, watery eyes from reading by lamplight. No more lonely evenings for widowers who could turn on a radio and hear plays and music. No more families dead from food poisoning when Ma could keep the potato salad in a chilly white refrigerator. No more heating sad irons on a blazing stove in August. The kids would stay on the farm.

He'd look at somebody with his round, clear eyes, he'd say, "If you put a light on every farm, you put a light in every heart." He never missed a day in four years, until the afternoon Diamond got killed trying to get a kite out of the lines.

Dad always left the house at five in the morning, carrying his lunch in a humped black lunchbox. A thermos bottle of coffee fit inside the top, held in place by a metal clasp. He and Diamond set poles and strung line to canted, ancient barns and to houses settled down on their foundations like old dogs sleeping on porch steps.

He got the idea they ought to carry a radio around in the truck. A farmer did his own wiring in those days, then called up The Icepick and said he was ready. Sometimes they had a washing machine hid under some burlap bags all set up to go as a birthday present for the wife. But usually just a couple of ceiling fixtures, outlets.

Before they turned on the power, Dad got his radio out of the truck, rubbed it up a little if it was dusty. He'd plug it in. There stood the farmer and his wife and the children, all staring at it.

"This is goin' to change your life," Dad would say.

He'd go to the window and signal Diamond to turn on the juice. As the static-rich sound of a braying announcer or a fox-trot poured into the room, he watched the faces of the family, watched their mouths opening a little as if to swallow the sound. The farmer would shake his hand, the wife would dab at her watery, strained eyes and say, "It's a miracle." It was as if my father had personally given them this wonder. Yet you could tell they despised him, too, for making things easy.

I never saw how anybody could rejoice over the harsh light that came out of them clear nippled bulbs.

After Diamond was killed Dad decided to go into the appliance business. That's what I do out in the barn. I was never able to do anything heavy. We still sell a few washers and electric stoves. Reba helps me get them onto the truck. There's not much in appliances now. It's all sound systems and computers. You can buy your washing machines anywhere.

At noon in summer, if they weren't too far away, Dad and Diamond would come back to the farm, drive up into the field and park the truck under the trees. They took the full hour. They had their favorite place. They'd spread out an old canvas tarp in the

shade. There was a spring up there. There was a slab of flat rock.
Sometimes Bootie or I would bring them up their dinner. We'd
skirt wide around Diamond, he'd make mocking kissing sounds
with his stained wet mouth.

Dad would laugh, "*Haw.*"

Sometimes Diamond was asleep with his shirt over his face so
the flies wouldn't bother him, and Dad would be on his knees,
tapping away at the rock with the chisel and the stone hammer
for something to do. Bootie and I could hear the *tok, tok-tok*
when we walked up the track. He was chiseling in the rock, chiseling out a big bas-relief of himself wearing his lineman's gear.
We'd play a kind of hopscotch on his grand design.

"Look, Dad," said Bootie, "I'm standin' on the eyes."

In the winter Dad and Diamond sat in the truck with the engine running.

The old family plot, not used for eighty years or so, is up in
back of the house. Diamond Ward is buried down in the Baptist
cemetery in Ironworks. *A Lamb of God Call'd Home, His Soul
No More Shall Roam.* Hey, we've seen that verse a hundred
times.

His eyes reflected a knowledge of his terrible mistake, my father told us. "He looked straight at me, his mouth opened and I
seen what I thought was blood, this dark trickle, come out. But it
was tobacco juice. He was dead there on the pole, lookin' at me.
I was the last thing he saw."

After Diamond was killed, Bootie and I played at the best
game we ever invented. We played it over and over for about two
years. Bootie thought up the idea of the molasses.

It wasn't so much a game as a play, and not so much a play as
acting out an event that gave us a sharp satisfaction. We'd get
some molasses in a cup and go out to the barn where we had our
things arranged. Pieced-out binder twine sagged between the
ladder to the hayloft and a crossbeam. We argued about who
would play Diamond first.

Bootie took her turn.

I'd say, "I'm Dad."

Bootie would say, "I'm Diamond." She would twist her face, hitch at her corduroy pants, kick at the floor.

"Hey, Diamond," I'd say, "there's a kite in the lines."

We'd look up into the dry twittering gloom. A kite hung there, as alert and expectant as a wounded bird.

"I'll get the goddamn thing out of our lines," said Diamond, taking up a long narrow stick. He climbed slowly, the stick hitting against the utility pole, *tok, tok-tok*. At the top Diamond turned and faced the kite.

"Be careful," I said.

The stick extended toward the kite, touched it.

5

A thin dust of snow falls. Visitors' cars rush along the road again, stirring up pale clouds.

"Must be havin' a party," says Aunt.

"Goodbye party, I hope," says Reba.

Mrs. Beaubien's little hungry face bobs into her window every time a car goes past.

Reba and Aunt and I get in the truck and go for a ride, careful to look straight ahead. There are eight coffee cans with dead marigolds on Yogetsky's porch. We can see the Moon-Azures up in the high field where the smooth, sloping granite lies exposed. We can see them among the poplars that have multiplied into a grove since I was a kid. Those trees all drop their leaves on the same day in autumn.

"That's the spring up there. Dad used to go up there at noon with old Diamond," I say. "Under the maple that went down."

"They can't be all that excited about a spring," says Aunt.

We see them bending over, one woman down on her knees with a pad of paper, drawing or writing. Dr. Moon-Azure leans forward from his hips with a camera screwed into his eye.

"They've got a body there," says Aunt. I can smell the faint lemony scent of lotion, the thick warmth of hair. The truck heater is on.

"More like a dead porcupine—probably the first one they ever see," says Reba. We turn around and go home and watch The Secret World of Insects. Our spoons clink and scrape at the cream and Jell-O in the bottom of the pressed glass bowls, the double-diamond pattern. It's just the field and the spring and the rock. Hey, I've been up there a hundred times.

The phone rings.

"What do you think," Marie Beaubien says.

"I think they've found a corpse in the bushes, one of those poor girls who'll take a ride from anybody in a red car," says Aunt.

"No, we would of seen that little skinny man, what's his name, over there in Rose of Sharon, the medical examiner."

"Winwell. Avery Winwell. His mother was a Richardson."

"That's right, Winwell. Yes, and the state police and all them. Whatever they've got there isn't no body."

"Well, I don't know what they could have found."

"Something."

The next day I walk down to Yogetsky's to get away from the sound of the vacuum cleaner. Reba knows it gets on my nerves.

Yogetsky is knocking the dead marigolds out of the coffee cans. Brown humps of dirt lie on the ground. He says, "See your neighbors found a Indian carving." I think at first he means the Beaubiens.

"What carving is that," I say.

"I got it inside in the paper," he says. I follow him into the kitchen. He washes his hands in the clean sink. The paper is folded over the arm of a chair. I look out the window and see our house, the grey clapboards stained with brown streaks from the iron nails, see the sign, CLEW'S APPLIANCES.

Yogetsky shakes out his paper until he finds the right place. He peers through his slipping glasses, his blunt finger traces across the text, and he reads aloud. "It says, 'Complex petroglyphs such as the recently discovered Thunder God pictured here are rare among the eastern woodland tribes.' It says, 'Discovered by the owners of a farm in Ironworks County.' " Yogetsky peers at me. "I didn't know there was no Indians around here."

He shows me the picture in the newspaper. I see my father's self-portrait cut deep into rock. In one stone hand he clenches three bolts of electricity. Around his waist is his lineman's belt. His hair flows back, his eyes fix you from the stone.

"Dad, I'm standin' on the eyes," said Bootie.

In our game the stick touched the kite, inexplicably fell away. Diamond swayed, his balance gone. Falling, his hand grasped the wire. His spine arched, his hand clenched living bolts of lightning. His eyes fixed mine, his mouth opened, and from the corner of his lips spilled the dark molasses, like blood, like uncontrollable tobacco juice.

I laugh, because isn't there something funny about this figure slowly cut into the fieldrock during the long summer noons half a century ago? And how can Yogetsky understand?

A Country Killing

TWO Jehovah's Witnesses, suffering in hot clothes, found the bodies a little before the cloudburst. They got out of their car, the man thin and sallow from some long trouble, stood a minute under the sawedged trees looking at the clouds coming up dark as plums, then at the trailer in the clearing. The man, arrowhead of sweat on the back of his suit jacket, hitched at his necktie, followed the woman up the path. The woman had experience. They had told him to stay in the background, watch how it was done.

The woman knocked at the door, the man behind her, holding his sunheated bible against his leg, breathing air as heavy as wet felt. The woman shaded her eyes with a plain hand, nails cut blunt; looked through the glass of the door and saw Rose lying faceup in front of the stove, saw a grimy brassiere in some huge triple-X size, and Rose's face with its raccoon's mask of bloody pulp. Warren was farther back, red foot and shin showing, the rest of him hidden by the stove. He had fallen against shelves crammed with empty jars, folded paper bags, spindles of binder twine. The smell of roasting chicken greased the humid air. The woman had to look at the stove, saw the oven knob set at 350. The man stared at Rose's pale pubic hair.

"Hello?" said the woman. "Are you all right?"

"They're dead. They look dead as mackerels."

The woman whirled, jumped past him down the steps, almost falling to her knees with the force of the leap, but rose again with the man limping after her, slapping his thigh for the car keys but still clenching the bible and some badly printed pages describ-

ing the future of the world and those in it. Lightning hair jolted
from the thunderheads.

The car swayed over the road, and before they entered the hair-
pin, raindrops the size of wild birds' eggs hit the windshield and
the trees roared over them, casting off twigs and whole branches.
The man drove through bursting rain and luminous blue hail that
sounded like an avalanche of gravel, and the woman's praying
voice burrowed under the drumming and thundercrack.

At the main road a washout cut them off from the blacktop.
On the other side they could see Sweet's Country Store. The
fogged windshield glowed like a television screen, rods of hail
and rain struck the macadam and rebounded in perpendicular
strokes; across the way the trembling letters that spelled out
BEER faded as the electricity died in the store. Suddenly the
man trod on the gas pedal and the car launched into the washout,
made it onto the blacktop before it stalled.

"We ought to get it off the highway."

He got out and pushed the car, and the woman pushed too, the
roadway water over the tops of their shoes, the woman's hair
twisting into snakelets, and the smell of dye coming out of their
drenched clothes. The red-coaled images of what they had seen
were already taking on ashy crusts, cooling into memory. They
ran for the store, splashing halos of water.

Inside, the woman shouted excitedly at Simone Sweet who
stood at the counter pumping up a gas lantern.

"Phone the police. People dead up there. In a trailer. Up that
road."

She spoke from the distance of the door, water draining from
her saturated hem. The overhead light flickered; the beer sign
glowed again. Simone pointed. The woman thought she meant
for them to go outside with their wet clothes, but, turning, she
saw the payphone and the man fumbling for a coin.

The store was in a river valley among scrolled cornfields that
broke green against sudden cliffs. The road ran along the river,

into the northern spruce, to Quebec. Because it went to Canada the road had a blue mood of lonely distances and night travel.

A spring ice jam had forced the river onto the road. The water, charged with branches and dead leaves, got into the store, gleaming like some brilliant wax, and ruined bags of potatoes, melted the labels off cans on the bottom shelves. For a few days farmers parked at the edge of the flood and sat in the cabs of their trucks, smoking and drinking beer, watching the slurring current. Someone said a drowned hog might have plugged a culvert. Finally a high school kid drove through the water, arm braced in the window, rooster tails spurting from the tires. One by one the watchers left, marking the macadam with muddy arcs as they turned around. The fogged cliffs buried their heads in rain; the dripping woods were as ill-defined as a grainy newspaper photograph.

The Sweets lived in a double-wide with awnings and picture window, set off by a scribble of fence and two plywood ducks. Their kitchen opened into the store. The side lawn was brown from close mowing. Albro rode the machine up and down every day, as though it were a horse that needed frequent exercise. At the center of the lawn were five boulders and an upended bathtub painted the bitter blue of a Noxzema jar. A madonna stood under the curve of the tub rim. In winter her crusted chin rested on snow and the boulders became humped penitents.

Simone, arms like dowels, a frizz of tea-colored hair, worked all hours in the store under the droning neons, surrounded by potato chips, candy, toilet paper, dry gas, adventure videos, the lottery machine. She made the brownies herself. Smell of the devil's hooves from the coffeepot beside the cash register. Under the counter she had a metal box of rolled quarters and a nail puller with a broken claw.

"What good'll that do you?" said Albro.

"You wouldn't care to get clipped behind the ear with it."

Albro's good looks had slipped over thirty-odd years to a

hump of steel-colored hair, a congealed expression, oily hands picking over a strew of metal parts. A silvery scar the size of a beer cap marked one thigh, from the time when he was married to his first wife and had fallen raving drunk into a barbwire fence after a jealous fight because she knew he was cheating with other women. That supple, hot-blooded self was still stored in his stiffening body, though long unused.

He was a night driver. A hundred times a year he eased open the door of the back room where he slept—the office they called it: a desk buried in bills and receipts, a cot, a tumble of blankets—while Simone slept in the double bed in the front bedroom in the bleed of the yard light, her shoes crooked on the rug in front of the bureau like dead fish on a sandbar.

Sometimes he was out until morning light. Simone would hear the loose rumble of the wrecker pulling in and get up to start the coffee. Albro, stinking of cigarettes, would lean his elbow on the table and tell her what he'd seen as he'd crawled on the sweet note of second gear over the moon-shot roads, pitted and obscure under the wheels.

"I see two bobcats fighting or fucking in a ditch, one, don't know which, anyway, blood on the fur."

Wailing songs on the radio. In the rainy headlights the side roads glistered like roof flashing. He came upon disabled cars wallowed in snow or drunks passed out on their steering wheels. If they wanted a tow, he charged thirty-five dollars. Once, he caught a glint in the roadside alders that turned out to be a ring hanging on a twig, a ring set with chip diamonds. And, years back, that car with Arizona plates in a snowplow turnaround, nose pointed into the woods and the windows frosted on the inside with condensed breath, the dead man dimly visible through the pearly scrim of his past exhalations. Fragments of teeth across his jacket like red crumbs.

"Come all that way to do it," said Albro.

Simone listened, spreading newspaper on the concrete floor, down on her knees to jab into the vending machine with a straightened coathanger.

"Supposed to be rodentproof, but there's a mouse in there. Must weigh three pound now off the candy. You ought to stay away from a car pulled off the road. Get mixed up in it. You don't know who's in it. You ought to be taking care of the mice and rats eating us up."

"Could be somebody needed a tow."

"Ask me, *you* need a tow."

How many times had he driven up Trussel Hill, the road bent like a folded straw before it went nowhere, seven or eight miles of uphill woods ending in Warren Trussel's yard with its chalky, rake-ended trailer up on blocks, the thirdhand kind from the back of the lot, the kind with a spaceheater between the bedroom and the door? The mobile-home salesmen, laughing in their plywood office, called them roaster ovens. Through the trees Warren's roaster oven resembled a sinking boat. Sometimes, when Albro pulled in, a mealy face loomed at the door, a flashlight ray stuttered over the lumber piles. Albro took his time turning around.

The trailer swam in a sea of junk auto parts, mildewed hay bales, cable spools, broken shovels and tractor seats, logging chains, the front half of a bus without windows or engine, a late-model wreck folded like a wallet. Plywood steps atilt, aluminum door decorated with a curlicued letter in stamped metal .22-shot into a twist.

"Prob'ly Warren done that," he told Simone. "Fed up to see that *B* every time he opens the door. *B* for bum. *B* for deadbeat. He made them halfassed steps. Only trailer in the world without a dog. *B* for sonofabitch."

"Don't know how anybody can live that way." Simone wiped the table, looked in Albro's coffee cup to see if he was done yet.

She knew Warren. When she opened the store Friday mornings he was there, tall as a henyard post, wearing brown canvas overalls that stood away from his legs like tarpaper rolls, nodding his big panhead with its greasy cap. Down for the mystery bins and his lottery ticket. Sore-looking eyes. He pawed through the boxes of cans without labels, the halfprice microwave dinners.

✼ ✼ ✼

"How can you tell how long to heat up them microwaves, Warren," said Simone in her pitched storekeeper's voice. "No way to tell how long to cook them if the labels is off."

"Guess at it. Can't tell what you get until you get it. Beans. Soup. Chinese shit. Cans is better. Know what the best ones is? Some a that dogfood. That is kangaroo. That is good meat. Too good for goddamn dogs." Heavy mouth with its frieze of cold sores, stubble over the jaw and down the neck into a fester of ingrown hairs.

He logged in winter if somebody came up with a short crew, in summer stacked boards at the lumber mill, picked up roadside bottles in company with Archie Noury. Sometimes he had a horse up by the woods for a few weeks, keeping it for somebody.

"Horses?" A farmer looked at Simone, his thick yellow hand on the counter a little in front of the quart of ice cream, three blackening bananas, a canister of ersatz cream. "Let me tell you something about Warren and horses. You know that old Dodge he drives, thing hangs down so low its tits drag on the ground. You could put your fist through the side of the door. Somebody didn't know no better give him two kids' ponies to keep while they went off. He went to pick them up. He's got this business rigged up there, a pole in the back to separate the ponies. Gets them in and takes off. On the interstate, doing fifty at most. Paper trucks on the way up to Quebec, semis going past him, sixty-five, seventy miles an hour. The ponies see them big tandems eighteen inches away. Warren gets to the bridge, they are over the water there, the ponies see the railing. A couple trailer trucks pass Warren. He claims one of them hit the airhorn. The ponies lose it, rear up and one kicks the tailgate. Tailgate falls off and the ponies go out on the road. At fifty miles an hour, hitting the concrete and the trucks coming up fast behind them. That happened three years ago. And that's Warren and *horses.*"

"Oh my god," said Simone who had heard the story many times. "Was they hurt?"

"Hurt! I guess they was hurt. Killed. They was killed. Guts

and blood all over the road. Traffic piled up. State trooper had to shoot 'em to put 'em out of their misery."

"Guess I know somebody's going to have banana splits after supper," she said. Knew something about him, too—that he'd been seen coming out of a restaurant men's room in another town, naked to the waist and blushing scarlet from belt-line to scalp. Shirt rolled up under his arm. Who could say what that was about?

On Father's Day Albro went to see his sons by his first wife, Arsenio and Oland, twenty-eight and twenty-six years old and still living in the Homer B. Bake Training Home. They would never be trained for anything but raking leaves or sweeping the long, shining corridors, their hairy arms scything away the years.

Arsenio never knew him, but Oland said, "Dad, Dad, Dad," like a mourning dove, whacking his pliant hands together in counterpoint. Unless it was raining, they stood on the lawn. Wooden benches faced each other like wrestlers. Arsenio's waxy fingers clenched his broom. Albro stood alone and to the side.

"Well, here's your dad again come to say hello and see how you're gettin' along," he said. Arsenio's face clenched like someone listening to a loudspeaker test. He began to sweep the sidewalk and Oland, without a broom, swept with him. Albro walked beside them in the grass, doggedly giving the year's news.

"There was a break-in at the store and at first we thought nothing was took. But a day or so later Simone see the shoelaces was all out. Somebody robbed the shoelaces. Imagine that. And there was a flood. Foot deep in the store. Elgood Peckox, you remember him, Oland, he give you apples when you was little, well he died. Seventy-two years old. Cancer of the bowels."

"Papple," muttered Oland.

At the end of half an hour Albro handed each of the men who were his sons a two-pound box of chocolates shrink-wrapped in red plastic. Arsenio, gripped by the passion of sweeping, let his box fall, but Oland tore the crimson covering and crammed the dark candies into his mouth. His eyes closed and a kind of ruined beauty shuddered over his face like the hide of a horse disturbed by flies. Although he tried to cramp it back, hopeless affection fluttered in Albro like a tic.

Before Rose came to live with Warren Trussel he went around with Archie Noury. Simone often saw them driving past in Warren's old truck, heading out to pick up bottles along the roadside for the deposit money.

"Can't be much of a business," said Simone. "They get, what, twelve, fourteen dollars' worth of cans, if they're lucky, for a full day of fooling around. Have to buy more gas for what they use up; that takes most of the money. They get two six-packs, get a pack of them generic cigarettes, and that's it. Six beers and ten cigarettes for a day's work. Reminds me you ought to get at them potholes in the parking lot, 'stead of fooling around with the mower."

"Don't know how somebody can live like that," mumbled Albro.

One of the Nourys was a pastry chef, another the principal of an elementary school in Massachusetts, but the others were brawlers, knifers, crazy log-truck drivers known for taking corners too fast, rolling the load and leaping clear, unhurt.

"That's a rat's nest of Nourys up in the eastern townships," a farmer said. "You look in your graveyards both sides of the border you'll find plenty of Nourys. Most of them got there the hard way."

Archie Noury had ginger hair, bloodshot eyes and a scar down the middle of his nose that made him say, "what are you starin' at?" He was greasily handsome, despite the scar, and bad-tempered. He glanced in windows and mirrors not out of vanity but to see whom he resembled, for his parentage was uncertain. A locket on a tarnished chain hung around his neck, tangled in his chest hair. No one knew what pictures were inside. Maybe Rose, maybe she knew.

In the thick summer darkness, window cranked down for the cool, Albro pulled into Warren's yard to turn around, to begin his homeward run. A parked truck blocked the way. He looked it over in the moth-shot headlight glare; an old bucket with a varnished board sign in the back window, CHEVY, the letters fashioned from popsicle sticks; a rack of maple poles with the bark still on; and two bumper stickers—one on the driver's side HIS, on the passenger side HERS. Then somebody came up beside him, pressed the mouth of a side-by-side 12-gauge into the soft flesh of his neck. He smelled vanilla, swiveled his eyes to see a huge woman with hair billowing around her head like crimped silk.

"You're the booger turns around in the driveway. Warren don't want you to do it. So you better get out of here. This is private prop'ty." A creeping flashlight beam came out of the trailer door, slid over them, lighting up her yellow flaring hair and Albro's surprised hands gripping the steering wheel. He couldn't say a word at first, got his voice back when she lowered the gun.

"Hell, I didn't know nobody lived up here, thought the trailer was empty. He should of said something. End of the town road, no place to turn around."

"Is now. He cleared out over there." She pointed across the road with her chin.

Albro backed across into a slot of stumps and rocks that chewed his tires, turned, passed the trailer. She was up on the steps, Warren holding the aluminum door open for her with his foot, his flashlight twitching. The bumper stickers on the Chevy truck blazed and he saw where she'd tried to scrape HIS off.

A mile or two down the hill he pulled onto a logging road, drove into the ash whips, stopped, turned off the motor and lit a cigarette. His hands trembled. He couldn't stop seeing the purple mouth like melted crayon, the yellow hair; he still felt the shot-gun's hard snout.

At first light he was drinking coffee in the kitchen, and Si-mone was mixing brownies for the store. The window fitted around a sky like milk. She tilted a bottle; a fragrance rose from the bowl.

"What's that!"

"Vanilla, same as I always put in." She looked at him. "When you gonna do something about Robichaud's garden tiller? Been settin' there for weeks and they come by twice, see if it was ready."

Friday morning Albro rode his mower around the lawn in wet heat, starting from a central point known only to him and work-ing outward in a spiral. The river lay between its banks like molten lead; the cornfields were as flat as wallpaper. A farm truck dragged past in a hot clatter. Around eleven the Chevy truck with the pole rack pulled in.

Warren Trussel jumped down from the passenger side and went into the store. The fat woman followed him, hair like cas-cading heat over her magenta dress, a huge bell of fabric. Two laps of the lawn, the mower vibrating under his buttocks, and Al-bro saw them come out, Warren with his box of mystery cans. The woman said something and he went back in. She stepped onto Albro's lawn, waited at the edge for him to come around.

He stopped the mower but kept it running. The engine's tremors shook his flesh. She came up to the machine. The smell of vanilla mingled with exhaust. He stared at the lawn as if his interest was grass. Warren came out of the store again, got in the truck, and bent forward, drank from a can.

"Didn't know you was the storekeeper's husband; thought you was some troublemaker. Warren says it's okay if you turn around in the yard. Says it's okay, do whatever you want."

From the corner of his eye he saw Warren drain the can and turn toward them, his head framed in the passenger window. Albro cleared his throat. Quickly the woman's hot, ringless hand went to his groin, squeezed. She walked back to the truck, her sheet of hair flashing in the sun like signals. He threw the mower in gear and finished the lawn before he went in the store. Simone was wiping out the refrigerator case.

"How do you like that?"

"What," said Albro.

"Who Warren had with him. I see her over there talking to you. You know who she is, do you?"

"No. She wanted to know what time it was." He held up his left arm with its stainless-steel watch.

"She's Archie Noury's wife. Rose Noury. Left Archie, come to live with Warren. For how long, who knows? What I call leaving the frying pan for the fire. There'll be trouble over it. Archie Noury will make trouble. I remember Rose at school, big fat thing even then, a big fat slob. Wish it would rain and cool things off."

"Sooner or later," he said. He fished in his pocket, came up with a dollar and a quarter and laid it on the counter. He took a brownie. For the smell of the vanilla. It was not enough. Later he sneaked a small bottle off the shelf and slipped it in his pocket.

Miles away Archie Noury was sharpening an umbrella spoke, whetting the points of his hunting arrows, throwing his deer rifle up to his shoulder and dry-firing, flinging a knife at a post, punching at his mirror image, whirling to hit the surprised air.

"Nobody pulls nothin' on Archie Noury!" he shouted. "You like that?" he yelled at the gouged post.

Hot, listless days went by. There was thunder in the night but no rain. Albro fooled with the garden, got the lawn down to stubble. He stayed home, watched the late programs with Simone, slept or didn't sleep in the back room.

Wednesday the white air shuddered with heat and the hazy

cornfields undulated. Simone had a fan going, the wash of hot air riffling the real estate guides on the counter. Albro was in and out between the store and the garage. He was messed up, a snake eating its tail. He couldn't think of anything but the hot, ringless hand, the big haunches under the dress. He couldn't stand the waiting until night when it might cool down.

After the late news Simone went to bed where she lay listening to the wawl of trucks on the road, the sound of water running into the bathtub. She was awake when he drove out of the yard.

He turned in the stump-pocked cut, drifted past the trailer and there was Rose, leaning against a pile of boards. His wet hands slid on the steering wheel. His chin was smooth, hair still damp; he wore clean underwear, the pastel yellow boxer shorts that Simone bought at Ames, three to a package. Rose was walking to him through the darkness.

"Hey, ain't it hot? What took you so long? Thought I was gonna see you before this." She was in the seat beside him, the interior light briefly on her face, the huge arm shawled in bright hair.

"Where you want to go?" He listened to the engine beating and turning.

"Nowhere. Just pull in behind my Chevy."

"Here?" He was appalled. "What about Warren?"

"Warren! He don't have nothing to do with it. Just park there, it's okay."

But he wanted to go to the old logging road, get in behind ash saplings. No sir, he said, he wasn't going to park in Warren's yard. In the trash and the dirt.

"C'mon," she coaxed. "It'll only take a minute."

A minute wasn't what he had in mind, either. He said nothing.

"Well, then, I'm goin' back inside," she said. The event, which for days he had imagined as a luscious, secret hour behind the leaves, rotted in her purple mouth. Everything was screwed up.

"All right." He jerked the truck up behind the Chevy. HIS.

HERS. He turned off the engine and the lights, trod the emergency brake pedal. She was at him, agile for such a fat woman. And it did take only a minute, ending with a burst of light, his wide-open eyes seeing a flash that illuminated a pile of logs and some chicken bones and eggshells raying from a burst garbage bag.

"What was that?" His numb mouth mangled the words.

She laughed. "Oh, prob'ly only Warren shinin' his flashlight around. Heat lightnin'." She was already out of the truck. "Maybe a car comin' up the hill. Maybe somebody comin' to turn around in the yard."

"Maybe Archie Noury," he said meanly. Seven minutes after he'd pulled up, he drove away. He was sorry he'd wasted the hot water on a bath.

By the time he got to the bottom of the hill, he was sure it had been Warren Trussel crouched on one of the lumber piles with a flashbulb camera he'd stolen somewhere. The thought of Warren made him sick. Dirty trash like that. Warren and Rose. He gagged.

Archie Noury started to drink the next morning. He began with a dreggy swallow of Old Duke from an almost empty bottle in the stifling shithouse, switched to warm beer at 7:30, found a quarter of a pint of cheap tequila in the glove compartment, then, at noon, drove down to the shopping mall, cashed in his deposit bottles and bought a fifth of Popov. The bank thermometer read 92. He drove with the bottle between his legs, the neck sticking up like a glass hard-on. He looked at himself in the rearview. "Bam," he said. "Bam, bam. Thank you, ma'am."

Albro couldn't get the mower started. He could hardly breathe the thick air. Around one o'clock he went into the store. "I got to go get a part for the mower," he said.

"If this heat don't break soon," said Simone. She regarded the shimmering road, the distorted shapes of passing cars and trucks. She started to say something else, but Albro was already outside, his hand reaching for the door handle on the truck.

He came back late in the afternoon under knobby blue thunderheads pulsing with lightning. His face was grey and sweaty; he wiped at his mouth as if he'd eaten fried meat.

"What's the matter," said Simone, "heat got you?"

"Nothing."

"Looks like we're going to get it."

He went out to the garage to work on the mower.

The Jehovah's Witness man could not dial the state police number, his hands were shaking so hard. He had thought he had things under control but this shaking had started. The woman took the quarter out of his hand, dialed, did the talking. After she hung up she bought a bottle of pop from Simone.

"The police cruiser is coming," the woman said and retold what she had seen, the fat naked body, the bloody foot; the roasting chicken, burned up by now; the heat, the washed-out road.

"We ought to pray," she said, looking at the man who stood off by himself, gazing into the rain. She put her chin down and folded her hands. "I believe in the love of Jehovah and its power to—come on, pray with me."

"I believe in love . . ." said the man.

Simone said she had to run over to the garage for a minute. She held a folded paper bag above her hair, dodged through the downpour.

Albro leaned against the edge of the workbench at the back of the garage, the oily fingers of his right hand pulling the fingers of the left. The bench was littered with tools and empty brown vanilla bottles.

"Well," Simone said, "there's two bible nuts, just come down from Warren Trussel's place. Say they are both dead on the floor. Called up the police."

❦ ❦ ❦

She squinted, and made out the blue bathtub and the madonna in the streaming rain through the window behind him. "It's really coming down." The cotton dress hung damp on her stick bones.

"Um," he said.

She sighed, walked over to the door and opened it.

"That's the cruiser. They got here fast enough." She held the damp newspaper over her head, ready to make a run for it. "Now I'm goin' to tell you something. You shut up. You hear me, you just shut up," she said.

He knew that much, anyway.

Negatives

YEAR after year rich people moved into the mountains and built glass houses at high elevations; at sunset when the valleys were smothered in leathery shadow, the heliodor mansions flashed like an armada signaling for the attack. The newest of these aeries belonged to Buck B., a forcibly retired television personality attracted to scenery. A crew of outside carpenters arrived in the fall and labored until spring. Trucks bearing great sheets of tempered glass crept over the dirt roads. The owner stayed scarce until June when his dusty Mercedes, with an inverted bicycle on the roof, pulled up at the village store and in came Buck B. clenching a map and asking for directions to his own house.

A few weeks later the first yellow cab ever seen in the town disgorged Walter Welter in the same place. Walter, who had come a long way in ten years from Coma, Texas, called Buck B. on the pay phone, said he was at the store and Buck B. could just get down there and pick him up. The cab driver bought a can of pineapple juice and a generic cheese sandwich, waited in his taxi.

"I give 'em a year," said the storekeeper peering out between advertising placards, watching Walter transfer tripods, portfolios, cameras and six suitcases from the taxi to the Mercedes.

"Tell you what *I'd* give 'em,'" said the tough customer. "What *I'd* do."

But it all was all over before the first snow and no one had to do a thing.

·   ·   ·

🦓🦓🦓

"Why do you let that slut come here?" said Buck, casting his lightless eyes on Walter, who knelt beside the tub in the downstairs bathroom. Buck's hands were crusted with clay, held stiff in front of his black apron. Walter's hands were in yellow rubber gloves, scrubbing away Albina Muth's greasy ring. Buck's face was all chops and long teeth like the face of Fernandel in old French comedies; his hair rippled like silver water.

"You think you're going to get some photographs, don't you? That she's some kind of a subject. The Rural Downtrodden. And then what, the pictures lie around in stacks. Nobody but you knows what they are. The edge of an ear. A dirty foot. You better keep her out of the upstairs." He waited but Walter said nothing. After ten or eleven seconds Buck kicked the bathroom door shut, stalked back to his clay, hands held in front of him like ceremonial knives shaped for cutting out viscera.

The fingers on both hands wouldn't count the dinners Walter Welter ruined with his stories of Albina Muth. Friends came up from the city for a mountain weekend, had to listen to grisly accounts: she had left her awful husband for a deranged survivalist who hid knives under tin cans in the woods; she lived with an elderly curtain-rod salesman made such a satyr by rural retirement that Albina had been rushed twice to the emergency room; she was being prosecuted for welfare fraud; her children had head lice; she sported a vestigial tail.

They saw her at the mall supermarket standing in line with children clustered on the cart like flies, or carrying bags of beer and potato chips out to a pickup truck in the parking lot. Her children, with thick-lidded eyes and reptilian mouths, sat in the bark-strewn truck bed rolling empty soda cans. Albina, her hair squashed against her head, climbed into the passenger seat of the cab, smoked cigarettes, waiting for someone who would come later.

One day Walter passed her walking on the muddy shoulder of the road, the children stumbling and squalling behind her. He pulled up, asked if she wanted a ride.

"Sure as hell do." Smoky, rough voice. She stuffed the kids with their chapped, smeared faces, into the back seat and got in beside him. She was thin, about the size of a twelve-year-old. Her coarse hair looked like she cut it herself with a jack-knife, her white face like a folded slice of store bread. He noticed, not the color of her eyes, but the bruised-looking flesh around them.

"Know where the Bullgut Road is? Next one after that's my road. You'n drop us there." The tone was bold. She bit at her nails, spitting fragments off the tip of her tongue.

The road was a skidder-gouged track. She pulled the half-asleep children out like sacks, saying, "come on, come on," and started up through the mud, one brat jammed onto her hip, the other two coming at their own pace and crying. He waved, but she didn't look around.

At dinner he did an imitation of the way she wiped her nose on the back of her hand. Buck B. listened, tarnished hair clouded with clay dust, eating his dish of yogurt and nuts, gazing through the glass wall at the mountain. He said, "God, that's beautiful. Why don't you do mountain studies? Why don't you take pictures of something attractive?" Then he said he was afraid that Albina Muth's children had sowed the back seat of the Mercedes with louse nits. They were starting to fight when the phone rang and Walter got the last word, saying, "I'm not here if it's one of your stupid friends wanting a tree picture." He meant Barb Cigar, who once had called to say that her trees were covered with lovely perfect leaves and didn't Walter want to come with his camera? No, he did not. It was Barb Cigar with the dewlapped mouth like the flews of a hound who had given Buck B. an antique sabre reputed to have fallen from Casimir Pulaski's hand in the battle for Savannah (a parting token from her ex-fa-ther-in-law from his cutlery collection), she who had sent a youth in a panda bear suit to sing Happy Birthday under Buck's window, she who named her Rottweiler puppy "Mr. B."

• • •

Walter Welter's photographs were choked down and spare, out-of-focus, the horizons tilted, unrecognizable objects looming in the foreground, the heads of people quartered and halved. What he called the best one showed a small, boxy house with a grape arbor and a porch glider. The grass needed cutting. Guests sorting through the photographs kept coming back to this dull scene until gradually the image of the house showed its secret hostility, the arbor turned harsh and offensive, the heavy grass bent with rage. The strength of the photograph emerged as though the viewer's eye was itself a developing medium. It would happen a lot faster, said Buck, if Walter wrote out the caption: *The House where Ernest and Lora Cool were Bludgeoned by their Son, Buxton Cool.*

"If you have to say what something's about," said Walter, "it's not about anything except you saying it's about something."

"Spare me," said Buck, "spare me these deep philosophical insights."

Walter's photographer friends sent him prints: an arrangement of goat intestines on backlit glass, a dead wallaby in a waterhole, a man—chin up—swallowing a squid tentacle coming out of a burning escalator, Muslim women swathed in curtains of blood. One of the friends called from Toronto, said he'd spent the summer with the archeologists flying over the north looking for tent rings. "There was this Inuit cache on the Boothia Peninsula." Distance twisted his voice into a thinning ribbon.

The wooden box, he said, fell apart when it was lifted from the earth. Inside they had found knives, scrapers, two intact phonograph records of religious music, a bullet mold, a pair of cracked spectacles, a cooking pot stamped *Reo,* needles, a tobacco can. From the tobacco can they took a dozen negatives, the emulsion cracked with age. Prints were on the way to Walter.

When they arrived he was disappointed. All but one of the photographs showed squinting missionaries. The other photograph was of an Inuit child in front of a weather-whitened building. Her anorak was sewn in a pattern of chevrons and in the crazed distance lay a masted ship. Her face had the shape of a hazelnut, the eyebrows curved like willow leaves. She leaned against the scarred clapboards, arms folded over her breast, mouth set in a pinched smile and both eyes lost in their sockets.

Walter caught the flaw in the shadow. Light coursed through the space between the soles of the child's boots and the ground because her weight was on her heels. She was propped against the building.

"It's a corpse," said Walter, delighted. "She's stiff."

Buck, toasting oatcakes, wondered what the photograph meant. "Like Nanook of the North, maybe? Starved to death? Or tuberculosis? Something like that?"

Walter said there was no point in trying to understand what it meant. "It can't mean anything to us. It only meant something to the one who put this negative in the tobacco can."

Buck, wearing a scratchy wool sweater next to his skin, said something under his breath.

Once or twice a week they drove to the mall with its chain stores, pizza stands, liquor store, sixty-minute photo shop, While-U-Wait optician, House of Shoes, bargain carpet, and Universal Herbals.

"I told you to bring the other credit card," said Buck. "I told you the Visa was ruined when it fell under the seat and you moved it back."

Walter pawed through his pockets. He leaped when Albina Muth rapped on the passenger window with a beer bottle. She was smiling, leaning out of a garbage truck parked beside them, smoke flooding out of her mouth, her rough brown hair like fur. She was wearing the same grimy, stretched-out acrylic sweater.

"Nice truck," cried Walter. "Big."

"It ain't mine. It's a friend of mine's. I'm just waitin' for him." She glanced across the highway where there were three low-slung bars: The 74, the Horseshoe, Skippy's.

Walter joked with her. In the driver's seat Buck invisibly knotted up, yanked himself into a swarm of feelings. He had found the other credit card in his own pocket. Albina threw back her head to swallow beer and Walter noticed the grainy rings of dirt on her throat.

"You take pictures?"

"Yeah."

"Well, sometime maybe you'n take one of me?"

"For god's sake," hissed Buck, "let's go."

But Walter did want to photograph her, the way she had looked that day by the side of the road, the light strong and flickering.

In October Albina Muth started to sleep in the Mercedes. Walter went out on Sunday to get the papers. There she was, so cold she couldn't sit up. He had to pull her upright. Dull, black-circled eyes, shivering fits. She couldn't say what she was doing there. He guessed it was a case of Saturday night drinking and fighting, run off and hide in somebody's car. It was a two-mile walk from the main road to somebody's Mercedes, and all in the dark.

He brought her into the house. The south wall, glass from roof to ground, framed the mountain, an ascending mass of rock in dull strokes of rose madder, brown, tongues of fume twisting out of the springs on its flanks. The mountain pressed into the room with an insinuation of augury. Flashing particles of ice dust stippled the air around the house. The wind shook the walls and liquid shuddered in the glass.

In that meaningful house Albina Muth was terrible, pallid face marked by the weave of the automobile upholstery, hands like roots, and stinking ragbag clothes. She followed Walter into the kitchen where Buck worked a mathematical puzzle and drank seaweed tea, his lowered eyelids as smooth as porcelain, one bare monk's foot tapping air.

"What?" he said, shooting up like an umbrella, jangling the cup, slopping the puzzle page. He limped from the room, the cast on his right foot tapping.

"What happened to him?" said Albina. She was attracted to sores.

Walter poured coffee. "He hit a deer."

"Didn't hurt the car none!"

"He wasn't in the car. He was riding his bicycle."

Albina laughed through a mouthful of coffee. "Hit a deer ridin' a bike!"

"The deer stood there and he thought it would run off so he kept on going but it didn't and he hit it. Then the deer did run off and Buck had a broken ankle and a wrecked bike."

She wiped her mouth, looked around. "This is some place," she said. "Not yours, though. His."

"Yeah."

"Must be rich."

"He used to be on television. Long ago. Back in the long ago. A kid's show—*Mr. B.'s Playhouse.* Before you were born. Now he makes pottery. That's one of his cups you're drinking from. That bowl with the apples."

She put her head on one side and looked at the table, the clay floor tiles, the cast-iron bulldog, the hand-carved cactus coat rack, drank the coffee with a noise like a drain and over the rim of the blue cup she winked at Walter.

"He's rich," she said. "Can I take a bath?"

What would she say, thought Walter, if she saw Buck B.'s bathroom upstairs with the François Lalanne tub in the shape of a blue hippopotamus? He showed her to the downstairs bath.

She came many times after that, walking up the private road in the dark, crawling into the car and filling it with her stale breath. Walter threw a sleeping bag in the back seat. She added a plastic trash bag stuffed with pilled sweaters and wrinkled polyester slacks, a matted hairbrush, pair of pink plastic shoes with a butterfly design punched over the toe. He wondered what she had done with her children but didn't ask.

In the mornings she waited outside the kitchen door until Walter let her in. He watched her dunk toast crusts, listened to her circular talk that collapsed inward as a seashell narrows and twists upon itself, and at noon when the bars opened he took her to the mall.

"Come on, take my picture. Nobody never took my picture since I was a kid," she said.

"Someday."

"Walter, she is living in my car," said Buck B. He could barely speak.

Walter threw him a high smile.

The deep autumn came quickly. Abandoned cats and dogs skulked along the roads. The flare of leaves died, the mountain moulted into grey-brown like a dull bird. A mood of destruction erupted when a bull got loose at the cattle auction house and trampled an elderly farmer, when a car was forced off the road by pimpled troublemakers throwing pumpkins. Hunters came for the deer and blood trickled along their truck fenders. Walter took pictures of them leaning against their pickups. Through binoculars Buck watched loggers clearcut the mountain's slope, and Albina Muth slept in the Mercedes every night.

Walter liked the road called Mud Pitch and drove past the wreck of the old poorhouse two or three times a week. This time it showed itself to him like some kind of grainy Russian nude tinted egg-yolk yellow. As he stared the sunlight failed and once more it became a ruined building. He thought he would photograph the place. Tomorrow. Or the day after.

A cold front rolled in while they slept and in the morning the light jangled through cracking clouds, the sky between the house and the mountain filled with loops of wind. The camera strap sawed into the side of Walter's neck as he ran down the terraces to the car. He could hear the bulldozers on the mountain. Albina Muth was curled up on the back seat.

❦ ❦ ❦

"I'm working today. Got to drop you off early."

The mountain mottled and darkened under cloud shadow. There was no color in the fields, only a few deep scribbles of madder and chalky biscuit. Albina sat up, face thickened with sleep.

"I'nt bother you. Just lay here in the car. I'm sick."

"Look. I'm going to be working all day. The car will be cold."

"Can't go back up to the trailer, see? Can't go to the mall. He's there, see?"

"Don't tell me anything about it." He cut the Mercedes too far back, put the rear wheels in Buck's spider lily beds. "Don't tell me about your fights."

The poorhouse was a rack of wind-scraped buildings in fitful sunlight, glaring and then dark like the stuttering end of a reel of film spitting out numbers and raw light. Albina followed him through the burdocks.

"I thought you wanted to stay in the car and sleep."

"Oh, I'n look around."

Inside the rooms were as small as pantries and closets. Furrows of clay-colored plaster had fallen away from the lath, glass spindled across the floor. The stairs were slides of rubbish, bottles, feathers, rags.

"You gonna fix this place up?" she said kicking nut husks, pulling light chains connected to burst bulbs.

"I'm taking pictures," said Walter.

"Hey, take my picture, o.k.?"

He ignored her, went into a room: punched-out door panels, drifts of flies in the corners and the paint cracked like dried mud. He heard her in another room, scratching in the filth.

"Come in here. Stand by the window," he called. He was astonished by the complexity of light in the small chamber; a wave of abrasive grey fell in from the window, faded and deepened along the wall with the swell and heave of damp plaster. She put

her arm along the top of the low window, embracing the paint-
less frame and resting her head on her shoulder.

"Just like that."

The light flattened so she appeared part of the window casing.

"For god's sake take that disgusting sweater off."

Her knowing smirk disappeared into the hollow of the rising
sweater. She thought she knew what they were about. Her mouth
ruched, she stood on alternate feet and kicked off her pants. She
was all vertical, downward line, narrow arms and legs like wood
strips, one nipple blank, erased by light, the other a tiny gleam in
the meagre shadow of her body. She waited for Walter to bite her
arms or shove her against the soiled wall. He ordered her to
move around the room.

"Now by the door—put your hand on the doorknob."

Her purpled fingers half-closed on the china globe. The dumb
flesh took the light from the window, she coughed, leaned
against the door and the paint fell in brittle flakes. But there was
a doggishness about her bent shoulders, her knuckled back, that
goaded him.

"Behind the door. Squeeze into that broken panel. Don't
smile."

Her face appeared in the splintered opening, washed with the
false importance the camera inflicts. *Click . . . whirr*

Walter's thrusting look swept the room across the hall; he saw
on the floor a mound of broken glass, splinters and curved blades
sloped in a truncated cone. Light pierced a broken shutter.

"Squat down over that pile of glass." A hot feeling rushed
through him. It was going to be a tremendous image. He knew it.

"Jesus, I could get cut."

"You won't. Just keep your balance."

Submissively she lowered herself over the glass, the tense, bitten fingers touching the dirty floor for balance. Spots of sunlight
flew across her face and neck as the clouds twitched along. She
filled the viewfinder.

Again the angled limbs, the hairy shadows and glimmering
flexures of her body.

❦ ❦ ❦

"Can I put my clothes on? I'm freezin'."

"Not yet. A few more."

"Must of taken a hunderd," she cried.

"Come on."

She followed along to the end of the poorhouse where green shelves pulled away, to the fallen door that led like a ramp into the world. He headed for an old kitchen stove with a water reservoir, rusting in the weeds. The oven door fell away when he grasped the handle. Albina hung back, contracted and shivering.

"Albina, pretend you're crawling into the oven."

"I want to git my clothes on."

"Right after this one. This is the last one."

"I'n wait for you in the car."

"Albina. You pestered me over and over to take your picture. Now I'm taking it. Come on, crawl into the oven."

She came through the weeds and bent before the iron hole. Her hands, her head and shoulders went into the stove's interior.

"Get in as far as you can."

The blackened, curved soles of her feet, the taut buttocks and hams, the furred pinch of sex appeared in the viewfinder. There was no vestigial tail. She began to back out as he worked the shutter.

"I wanted you to take pictures of me smilin'," she said. "Thought they was goin' to be cute, I could get like a little gold frame. Or maybe like sexy, I could put them in a little black fold-up. Not gettin' in no stove, behind stickin' out."

"Albina, honey, they are cute, and some are sexy. Just a few more. Come on, stand in the hot water thing on the side there."

She climbed up onto the stove top, saying something he couldn't hear, stepped into the water reservoir. In a cloud of rust her feet plunged through the rotten metal. The top of the range was even with her waist, and she looked as though she were to be immolated in some terrible rite. Blood ran down her foot.

Helpless, dirty laughter spurted out of the corners of his mouth and Albina wept and cursed him. But yes, now he could squeeze that hard, thin thigh, pinch the nipples until she gasped. He thrust her against the stove. Later, when he dropped her at the bar, he gave her two twenties, told her not to sleep in the car any more. She said nothing, stuffed the money in her purse and got out, walked away, the plastic bag of clothes bumping against her leg.

Milky light spilled out of the house. Buck's shadow was limping back and forth, bending down, lifting, its shape distorted by run-neling moisture on the windows. Walter went in through the side door, down the back stairs to the basement darkroom.

The film creaked as he wound it onto the reel. He shook the developing tank, stood in the sour dark listening to the slip and fall of water, watching the radiant hand of the clock. The listless water slid away, he turned on the light. Upstairs Buck walked back and forth. Walter squinted at the wet negatives, at the white pinched eyes and burning lips, the black flesh with its vacant shadows, yes, a thin arm crooked down, splayed fingers and the cone of glass that looked like smoldering coals. He really had something this time. He went upstairs.

Buck stood against the wall, hands behind his back. On his good foot he wore a brown oxford with a thick sole. There were all of Walter's suitcases at the door.

"It's getting too cold," Buck B. said, voice like a ratchet click-ing through the stops.

"Too cold?"

"Too cold for staying here. I'm closing the house up. Tonight. Now." He had another house in Boca Raton, but Walter had never seen it.

"I thought we were going to stay for the snow."

"I'm selling it. I've put it on the market."

"Look, I've got negatives drying. What am I supposed to do?" He tried to keep his voice level in contrast to Buck's which was skidding.

"Do whatever you want. But do it somewhere else. Go see Al-bina Muth."

"Look—"

❦ ❦ ❦

"I'm sick and tired of having a tenant in my car. The Mercedes actually smells, it stinks, or haven't you noticed? The car is ruined. I'm sick and tired of listening to Albina Muth suck up my coffee. And I'm tired of you. In fact, you can have the car, the stinking car you ruined. Get in it and get out. Now."

"Look, this is ironic. Albina Muth is not coming back. She took all her stuff out of the car. This was it. Today. I took some pictures and that was it."

Buck B. looked toward the black window, toward the mountain drowned in the canyon of night, still seeing the slope stripped of trees, strewn with rammel and broken slash, and beyond this newly cleared slope another hill and the field with the poorhouse visible for the first time through the binoculars.

"Get out," he said through his nose, limping forward and raising Barb Cigar's ex-father-in-law's sabre. "Get out."

Walter almost laughed, old Buck B. with his red face and waving a Polish sabre. The Mercedes wasn't a bad consolation prize. He could have the interior steam-cleaned or deodorized or something. All he had to do was run back down the stairs, get the negatives and exit, this way out, one way to the Mercedes. He tried it.

About E. Annie Proulx

E. ANNIE PROULX lives in Vermont and Newfoundland, but spends much of each year traveling North America. She has held NEA and Guggenheim Fellowships and residencies at Ucross Foundation in Wyoming. Her short story collection, *Heart Songs and Other Stories,* appeared in 1988, followed in 1992 by the novel *Postcards,* which won the 1993 PEN/Faulkner Award for Fiction. The 1993 novel *The Shipping News* won the *Chicago Tribune*'s Heartland Award, the *Irish Times* International Fiction Prize, the National Book Award, and the Pulitzer Prize.